The Private Eye Five

Written by: William Bontrager

With: Heddrick McBride

Illustrated by: HH-Pax

Edited by: Ashante Webson

Edited by: Maureen Lunn

The Private Eye Five

Copyright© McBride Collection of Stories

ISBN-13: 978-1514190531

ISBN-10: 1514190532

The Private Eye Five

Chapter 1
Bubble Gum on the Camera

"Wow! I can't believe that I am going to meet Mystic Bradley," Donell happily pronounced.

He kicked down the street with his buddy, Fitz, which is short for Fitzpatrick.

Donell adjusted his backwards hat and smiled at the heavier Fitz. The two kids stopped while waiting for traffic. Big trucks and small cars alike beeped their horns impatiently. Donell spun his basketball on his finger.

Fitz stooped and tied his shoe tightly. The street was busy—Fitz didn't want to trip on his laces crossing the street. Smog rose in the Baltimore sky. Donell wiped his glasses on his shirt and smiled, seeing the foggy spots in his lenses disappear.

"What makes Mystic so special Donell?" Fitz asked. He double knotted his shoes like his mother always warned.

"Are you kidding? Mystic can do it all on the court! He can dribble around people until they're so dizzy they no longer see straight," Donell happily exclaimed, leaning on his buddies' shoulder.

"Can he score?" Fitz asks.

"Can he score? If you call averaging 35 points a game scoring! And he can jump higher than anyone, and stop on a dime. Look!" Donell exclaimed.

The street light blinked to say walk, so Donell, explaining how his favorite basketball player performs, stopped in the middle of the road, making his sneakers squeak, and pulled up for a jump shot over Fitz. His basketball rose in the air before Donell raced around his friend to catch it.

"He shoots! He scores! Mystic Bradley shoots over his opponent!" Donell cried out, sounding like a television announcer.

Fitz, moving a little slower, grins. His metal braces glint in the sun.

"Yeah well, his opponent is tired from playing Revenge of the Wood Elves until late last night," Fitz chuckled.

"Not me. Mystic always tells us that we need a good solid seven hours of sleep," Donell boasted as they cross.

"The Winged Night Bird says that crime never sleeps, and neither does Fitz," Fitz replied.

This made them both laugh. The Winged Night Bird is a comic book favorite for both boys.

They crossed the street and headed towards an area where there are many little shops. The air was crisp and chilly. People were already bundled up in sweatshirts and heavy jackets.

All of a sudden, a finger tapped Donell on the shoulder. When Donell turned, a girl with pigtails sprung to the opposite shoulder then playfully ducked behind a trash can to escape his sight.

"I see ya Lily," Donell said, and placed his hands in his pockets nonchalantly.

"That is only because I wanted you to see me, Donell. I was invisible until I pushed back my cape," Lily replied and raised her eyebrows.

'What's with that cape Lily? You look like a level 2 mage," Fitz said.

"Try level seven-thousand! I have just come from Donny's Party Store and I have become a most powerful magician," Lily exclaimed.

She was wearing a cape and tall hat with stars while holding a wand that looked like a tree branch. She also had a little shopping bag full of things that rattle back and forth when she moved. The shopping bag was tied around her waist so she could reach in and pull out her items quickly.

"You can't just buy stuff and say you are a magician, Lily. It takes some practice," Donell told her good-naturedly, tossing his basketball in the air.

"How do you know that I didn't go into another dimension, Donell? Maybe I went to a place where time stops completely and trained for thousands of years," Lily cried out before stomping her feet.

"Ok, Lily the Great. Calm down. We believe you. Do you want to hang with us?" Donell asked.

"I sort of wanted to go home, I mean, to my secret lair, and learn some more tricks," Lily hesitated.

"A group of wanderers need a high ranking sage to warn of danger and cast healing spells during conflict, Lily," Fitz added, his hand rubbing his chin.

Lily grinned widely at that, her eyes twinkling.

"Okay. Sure! I wouldn't want to explain to your parents you were turned into moldy bread because I wasn't there. Where are we going anyway?" Lily asked as they wove through the busy street.

"Only to see the great magician of the basketball court, Mystic Bradley," Donell happily announced.

Lily rolled her eyes. She didn't care much for basketball.

On the way there, a blur streaked across their path.

An excited voice followed it.

"Hey, Donell!"

It went past them in a flash. Then it circled back around the group as four hard wheels scuffled on the concrete.

It was a thin girl on her skateboard. She jumped up the curb, popping her board in the air and rolling past them.

"What's up Peg? Where are you off to?" Donell shouted out. He had to raise his voice because she was wearing earphones and listening to fast loud music. Her head was bobbing swiftly with the tempo of the music.

She turned sharp on her skateboard, avoiding hitting a brick wall. Then, she rode up the bricks before landing next to Donell, Fitz, and Lily. She came to a stop and yanked her earphones down.

Peg was dressed as usual in a torn sweatshirt. Her green hood was pulled up over her long red hair. She smiled and wooped happily at seeing her friends.

"Dudes, did you see that? I popped at the last second and rode that wall like a wave, man! Oh, I'm so stoked!"

Peg talked loudly but jumbled her words sometimes, making two words sound like one long one. But it was not hard for them to read Peg's expressions. All of the kids knew she was excited about a new trick and happy to see her friends. She hugged Fitz and high-fived Donell.

Then she spotted Lily and broke out in laughter. She tugged playfully at the bottom of Lily's cape.

"Lily, look at you dude. You look awesome, ha-ha," Peg laughed.

"And powerful," Lily pointed out with her wand.

"Where are you going Peg? You want to roll with us?' Donell asked as Peg popped the board up and caught it in her hand. She was scuffed up with scraped knees and dirty hands but happy and smiling.

"After you guys check my latest trick. Come on!" Peg cried out.

She jumped back on the board before getting a response. She wheeled down the street, weaving through people. To see if her friends were following, she looked back with a toothy grin over her freckled face.

"Come on come on," she called out, laughing. She rubbed her hands together, unable to hold in her enthusiasm. She performed a trick over some wet cement while waiting and landed with skinny legs and sneakers back on the board.

The kids followed her.

Donell couldn't help but notice that they were headed in

the direction where Mystic Bradley would be signing autographs. He anxiously checked his watch.

"Mystic Bradley will be at the Fit n Foot in half an hour," Donell reminded them all.

Lily and Fitz both came to a stop. Fitz held his hand to his mouth in surprise.

"Whoa! Not there. We will be made fun of Donell. You led us into a trap," Lily stopped and waved her wand ominously!

"I agree with Lily, Donell. The chances we avoid taunts and bullying are slim to none. I don't want to go now. I just remembered that I have some dishes I need to wash at home," Fitz's voice wavered.

The Fit n Foot was a shoe store run by Mr. Shultz and wasn't Donell's favorite store to go to either because some of the teens who hung out there were not friendly to them. Especially a tall, gangly eighth grader named Marcus. He went out of his way to make them miserable. Marcus worked there on weekends and after school.

He played sports with Donell but didn't like when Donell scored a point in soccer, or hit the ball in baseball, or made a jump shot in basketball. He also did not like Donell's friends. He thinks they were all weird.

The Private Eye Five

But to see Mystic Bradley and get an autograph, Donell could endure being teased by Marcus and his friends.

"Hey listen, guys. You don't have to go there with me. Nobody is stopping you from turning around. I'm the only fan of Mystic Bradley's here. We'll catch up later," Donell said and gave them a strained smile.

But Donell dropped his head as he walked away from his friends. Sometimes it was nice to have your good buddies by your side for something you were looking forward to. It made it all the more special. He started dribbling his basketball down the street, following Peg who was listening to her music again.

"You better go with him, Lily. He needs a magician to heal him if he gets hurt," Fitz told Lily.

"You should go, Fitz. Any dangerous adventure needs a quest leader. Nobody has more experience in quests and dangers then Ranger Fitz of the wild realms," Lily nudged him.

Fitz sighed. Lily had used Fitz's official online gaming title. That made it very hard for Fitz to walk away.

"Only if you go too, Lily because he needs us both," Fitz added.

"Okay, and if Marcus tries anything, I'll use my magic." Lily blurted, hesitantly following Fitz.

"And I will try begging and pleading," Fitz remarked.

"Hey Donell, wait up." Lily called out, running past Fitz to join Donell and being careful not to step on her long cape.

The two rejoined Donell and followed Peg as she skated off in front of them. Donell smiled and slapped Fitz on the back happily.

"It'll be fun you guys. Don't worry," Donell exclaimed. He was relieved to have his friends beside him again.

The street was busy, with people bouncing from block to block. However, Peg enjoyed skateboarding and knew all of the shortcuts. The gang followed her down back alleys to avoid the walkways and foot traffic. They approached an area where Peg stopped. She grinned under her shaggy red hair and hood.

The kids followed Peg directly behind the Fit n Foot shoe store. Since it was the back way, their view was blocked from the main street.

On the left, there was a green dumpster and a shiny yellow bin that was there for recycling old shoes. It sat in the grass just on the edge of a small concrete patch.

Donell checked his watch. It was 12:30 p.m. on a Saturday. In half an hour, Mystic Bradley was going to be around front.

In the meantime, he wanted to show support for his friend, Peg.

"Ok, Peggy, shred it dude," Donell yelled happily and clapped his hands.

She nodded to Donell and put a stop sign top over a cinderblock. It was next to a small set of steps where there was a steel handrail leading down.

"Ok, watch this. I call it my rail-buster!" Peg screamed excitedly. She ran with her board in her hand. She got to the concrete patch and put the board down on the ground and hopped on. This gave her enough speed to roll over the stop sign, which acted as a ramp.

She rolled up the sign, then jumped with her board under her feet. The kids marveled as Peg launched high in the air. She hollered excitedly while she was in the air before she latched on the handrail with her wheels. She went down on the rail swiftly, leaning back and balancing. The handrail made a screeching noise.

When she reached the end, she popped off the rail and landed!

Donell and the kids cheered. Peg yelled and pumped her fist in the air. She dashed to them and hugged them, chattering excitedly.

"Wow Peg! Nice job. I know you practiced that a lot since you stopped trying to do your bone-breaker 360 trick," Donell said to her.

"Why'd you stop practicing that trick?" Lily asked her.

"Because I could only get the bone breaking part down and not the 360," Peg laughed and waved her little finger that was wrapped up in a thick bandage.

"Well, I would say, based on your speed and the projection and angle of the stop sign, you could have completely leaped over the whole rail," Fitz added and smiled in Peg's direction.

"I don't know what that means but I think you dug it too." Peg cackled.

"Great job Peg. Why did you choose this place to try your trick though? There are plenty of better spots that have steps and a handrail," Donell said.

"I chose this place because I can't get chased out of here. Check it out, man," Peg said to them.

She pointed to the camera over the back door of the Fit n Foot. They all looked up, seeing a purple sticky substance all over the lens of the camera.

"Yuck," Lily grunted.

"Smart though," Donell added.

"There is no way for old man Shultz to catch me skating as long as that goop stays up there," Peg laughed.

Fitz strolled up the steps and used the end of a broom to poke the substance on the camera.

"Watch it Fitz. It might come alive like the blob monster," Lily warned.

"This is very interesting; It is grape bubble gum, and it is still wet," Fitz said.

"That means someone stuck it up there recently, but why?" Donell asked.

"I don't know. I was just skating by this morning and saw it and said, wow…this is the place to do my rail-buster," Peg said.

"And you noticed that? Man, Peg, when it comes to skateboarding, you have the eyes of an eagle," Donell said as he checked his watch.

"Hey guys, I have to get around front. I want to catch Mystic Bradley as he is going in the door," Donell told them.

"We will join you Donell. But let's hope Marcus is on his usual two hour candy bar break at Burp A-Lot," Fitz joked.

"After mastering the rail, I'm not scared of anything. Let's see what's up!" Peg yelped excitedly.

The group left the back of the store where the purple bubble gum was drying on the camera lens, squishy and wrinkly.

Chapter Two

Lily's Coin Trick

What the kids saw surprised them.

They arrived at the front of the store and saw the elderly owner in a panic. There were many kids with posters, jerseys, and shoes for Mystic to sign, leaving sadly. Their parents were leading them away trying to calm them. The owner of the store, Mr. Shultz paced back and forth in the doorway.

He was a short, stocky bald man with a crooked nose who talked with his hands emphatically. He was muttering to himself over and over and shaking his head rigorously.

"What is going on, Mr. Shultz?" Donell asked.

"Nothing, Donell, except that the great day we have planned for the kids is ruined," Mr. Shultz sighed.

Donell, Fitz, Peg and Lily stared at each other in shock.

Donell felt a dry pit forming in his stomach and throat. He

had been looking forward to this day for weeks.

"How is it ruined?" Fitz enquired.

"It's ruined because I have the worst luck in the world!"

Mr. Shultz cried out.

He threw his hands up to the sky.

"Now I have to call Mr. Mystic Bradley and tell him the

horrendous news," Mr. Shultz moaned.

He plopped down on the curb and reached for his phone.

"Wait, Mr. Shultz. First, tell us what happened. Maybe we

can help you," Donell said.

"Cheer up, sir," Peg remarked.

She skated over to him and handed him her dirty

handkerchief. He grabbed it without looking and started

dabbing his brow with it.

"Well kids, if you must know. Mystic Bradley was going

to show up here today to sign autographs and raise money

for the charity he is involved with. It is a wonderful charity that promotes literacy for children. It supplies books that teach good practical life lessons," Mr. Shultz said to them.

"Intriguing and delightful," Lily piped in.

"To raise the money, Mystic would donate his pair of Bradley Big Air Sneakers. He wore them when he scored the game winner last year. The shoes were delivered to me this morning through his assistant," he said.

"After the autograph signing, the shoes were going to be auctioned off. We had customers who would have given a lot of money to buy his sneakers to help out his charity," Mr. Shultz said as he wiped his eyes with the handkerchief, stifling back tears on his droopy face.

Then he abruptly sniffed the handkerchief, wrinkled his nose, and kindly handed it back to Peg who put it back in her pocket.

"So this morning I put the shoes on the center display. I had some papers to sign but after that, about an hour ago, I went to put on a fresh coat of cleaner on them, and I

saw…these instead," he moaned.

Mr. Shultz held out a pair of Bradley Big Airs and showed

the kids. They were black and white with a bright red

lightning streak on the sides.

"I don't see the problem," Fitz stated.

"I do," Donell spoke up, stepping toward Mr. Shultz.

"These aren't the ones that Mystic Bradley sent to Mr.

Shultz this morning. The older editions that Bradley wore

in Game 7 to hit a fade away as the clock was winding

down had a red stripe on the left foot. That was his quick

step foot. But these have the red stripe on the right foot,

which are the newer shoes, is that right Mr. Shultz?"

Donell asked as he looked at the shoes.

"You are sadly correct," Mr. Shultz nodded.

"That means that somebody replaced them?" Lily asked.

"That means someone stole them," Peg shouted.

"I bet it was Marcus," Donell cried and pounded his fist into his palm.

'But I was at the counter the whole time Marcus was in the store. I checked all of the cameras before I sent all my workers home for the day. The cameras showed nothing suspicious," Mr. Shultz told them.

"Then what happened to them?" Fitz questioned, rubbing his chin in deep thought.

"Maybe when I received them, I didn't use a security tag and someone walked off with them...Maybe I didn't have them all along. Maybe I am going crazy. I am in such a poor, poor, state. How could I lose those shoes? Oh I just don't know. Oh dear, oh dear," Mr. Shultz wept in his hands.

Donell frowned and crossed his arms. One thing he always knew Mr. Shultz to be was detailed. Just looking at his store proved that everything was always neat and in its proper place. That was why he was always wondering why he would let someone as lazy and unorganized as Marcus keep working there.

"Something is not right," Donell muttered.

"Hey Mr. Shultz, Marcus can be crafty. Can we look around in your store and see if we can find any clues?" Donell asked.

Mr. Shultz slowly removed his hands from his face. He sighed and lowered his shoulders.

"Kid, I checked everywhere but if you want to waste your time and Mystic's, then go right ahead," Mr. Shultz uttered.

"If we get back those shoes in time, Mystic can still show up and you can raise the money for the charity," Peg yelled, jumping on her skateboard and rolling into the store.

Lily closed her eyes and waved her hands.

"Maybe my magic will be able to give us a glimpse into the past. We might be able to see the crime before it happened," Lily added and reached inside her bag of tricks.

"This is no time to play around Lily," Donell snapped at her, distracted by his own thoughts.

Lily frowned and put her head down. She took her hand out of the bag and lingered behind as her friends all went into the shoe store. Mr. Shultz got off the curb and followed them in. He was not hopeful that a bunch of kids could find the missing shoes.

"Mr. Shultz, can me and Fitz look at the cameras and see what we can find?" Donell asked.

"I looked at them already and got zero. However, I'll take you upstairs to the camera room if that will please you," Mr. Shultz sighed.

"Thank you Mr. Shultz. I am well versed with video surveillance equipment," Fitz added.

None of them saw Lily as they disappeared into the Fit n Foot.

As they left, Lily turned and walked slowly in the other direction. She looked down at her feet as she went. She wished she could shrink herself and jump in one of the cracks in the concrete.

"I don't need those guys anyway. I'll just go home and turn my cat into a frog or something," she mumbled, and kicked a can down the street.

"Hey!" A voice rang out.

It came from the alley.

Lily watched an old man emerge. He was wearing a dark brown wrinkled hat with a long grey beard that drooped down to his knees. A jug of water sloshed around, tied to his waist with a rope. He smiled widely.

"Hey. Thanks for the can, kid. I can get six cents apiece for these," he said to her cheerfully.

He leaned down and snatched up the can. With a chipped smile, he tossed the can behind his back and kicked the can into a shopping cart. It went in with the other cans making a rattling noise.

"Cool! You didn't even have to look when you did that," Lily blurted.

"I used to play soccer with the King of Venezuela," the bearded old man said to her.

"Neat! It was almost like you made the can vanish," Lily cried.

"Are you a great magician, madame?" The old man asked her, glancing at her star cape and magic bag.

"Sure am! Well, I am learning. I can disappear with my cape but only for a few seconds. I need some more practice I guess," Lily said.

The old man bowed low, removing his hat.

"I am honored to be in the presence of a powerful magician in training. My name is Dices," the old man croaked.

"I am Lily. Thanks. I wish my friends appreciated my magic like you do. Donell thinks I am just being silly," Lily said to him.

The old man cocked his hat and smiled.

"I know how you feel, Miss Lily. But don't let that get you down. If he is a true friend he will appreciate you for your special qualities. You seem to be very imaginative and he will see that. Give him a chance, Miss Lily," Dices warmly instructed and shuffled over to his shopping cart full of cans.

"Sure. Okay. Thanks Dices. I guess I can try. Donell really wanted to see his favorite basketball player—now he can't," Lily said.

"Then maybe he was just upset. Lots of luck," the old man called out and went back in the alley rolling his shopping cart. He whistled a tune as he left.

Lily turned and headed back to the shoe store. She wished to help her friends as much as possible. She wanted to see Donell get to meet his sports hero, and also see that Mystic's charity got the money.

When she got back to the shoe store, Peg was looking under all of the seats, behind the mirrors, in the trash cans, behind the counter, on top of the television set bolted to the wall, and even taking posters off and looking behind them for a secret compartment. While she searched, she was singing loudly to herself with her earphones on.

Lily came over to her and shouted, but Peg didn't hear her.

Peg raced behind the counter and pulled up the carpet there. She looked under it, and found nothing but dust. It kicked up in a great dark cloud that made Lily cough. Peg slammed the carpet down and turned, beaming once she spotted Lily.

"Hey dude! Where'd you come from? I have been looking everywhere for these shoes. But, I haven't checked this big poster yet. Here Lily! Help me get it down," Peg rambled and went over to the wall where a big poster was stuck on the wall with tacks.

Before Lily could react, Peg reached for the poster and ripped it straight down the middle.

"SHHHRIPPPP!"

The middle piece of the poster fell down in shreds at her feet.

"Oops. That's major carnage," Peg muttered.

"Let's see what's behind it," Lily told her. There was no use to get mad at Peg now. The poster was already torn up. The best thing to do was to go with it.

They looked behind the poster but there was only an egg colored wall there.

"Nope! Nothing," Peg grimaced and tried to think how she could fix the tear in the poster.

"What did you hope to find anyway, Peggy?" Lily nudged.

"I saw a movie once where this dude escaped through a wall behind a poster. He dug a tunnel and everything. It was cool. I thought the thief could have done that too," Peg said.

Lily imagined Marcus, hunched down in the tunnel,
behind the poster, waiting for everyone to leave. Then he
would burst through the poster and leave with the shoes
when it was dark outside.

With thoughts of secret passageways and magic bubbling
up in her head, it was hard for Lily to keep focused on
practical things—the stolen shoes.

Instead, she suddenly remembered what she bought at the
magic store.

The matchbox and coin trick, Lily thought, getting
excited. She remembered wanting to try the trick out before
she saw Donell and Fitz.

"Hey Peg. Do you want to see a trick? I think I can do this
one," Lily said.

"Yeah Lily! Go for it. Don't tell Donell though. He is
super serious right now," Peg whispered.

"Okay. Here goes, Peg. Watch and be amazed," Lily
proclaimed, waving her wand!

Lily pulled out a simple box of matches from her bag. She opened the matchbox and poured all the matches out on the counter. They were toy matches that she got at the trick store. They all were rubber and bounced on the counter in a spongy heap. But Peg only saw that the matchbox looked real. Her eyes got big.

"Lily! Setting fire to the store is no magic trick. My Uncle Jim did that to a fruit stand and he is no magician," Peg whispered, watching all the matches pour out of the box.

"I am not Uncle Jim. I am Lily the great! Observe casual audience member, that there is no coin in this matchbox," Lily announced to her.

"Yeah dude. It is empty. Some trick," Peg said looking in the matchbox, and craning her head to see the inside of the box.

"Now I will amaze you. I will close the box and when I say the magic words…you will see a shiny silver coin in the box when there was not one before."

"Alright," Peg said.

Lily whispered the magic words and waved her wand.

"Hear me clear, coin appear," she shouted.

Then she opened up the matchbox and Peg saw the shiny coin, resting on the bottom of the match box.

Peg's eyes widened.

"Whoa! That was incredible! Lily you are awesome!" Peg shouted.

This caused Donell to scamper down the steps. He looked at the two girls hoping they discovered a clue. Instead, he saw the bunch of toy fake matches on the counter and Lily's magic bag scattered on the floor. He also saw Mr. Shultz's poster is ripped in two. All of this caused Donell to shakes his head. He frowned at them before racing back upstairs to the camera room.

"Wow! Donell seems real upset," Peg whistled.

"I'm sorry. I got so carried away with my magic," Lily said to Peg with sadness.

"How did you do that trick? It was awesome," Peg leaned in.

"It's a secret, but I'll let you in on it. Just you! Before I pour the matches out, I place the coin inside, on the edge, under the lid, like this," Lily told Peg.

She slipped the coin in the top corner of the box of matches, but not so much that the coin fell inside.

"So it is hanging there the whole time," Peg cackled.

"Yes. Then when I push the lid shut, it pushes the coin in the box. Then I open the lid and there is our coin," Lily laughed.

Peg cheerfully slapped Lily on the back.

"Wow Lily! That is great!" Peg smiled.

"You were talking about secret passage ways and I remembered that. A secret passageway keeps things unseen even though it is close by. I guess I got carried away with it though. Now Donell really thinks I am playing around,"

Lily sadly gathered up the fake matches, the coin, and the box.

"Hey Lily. It's cool. Donell will love your trick too. No worries," Peg said and went back to thinking about the location of the missing shoes.

Lily smiled at that idea, and thought about Dice's advice to her. She was very imaginative and there were many ways that she could be of use in this case.

The Four Cameras

Chapter 3

"Those girls are fooling around downstairs," Donell said disgustedly.

"Don't worry Donell. In my experiences among the rugged online terrains and perilous mountains, a wizard and a warrior are keys to having a successful mission," Fitz exclaimed.

"This isn't a computer game, man! Am I the only one that is taking this seriously?" Donell threw his hands up in the air.

"Donell, we all are. That is why I am looking at these surveillance cameras. We all want to help you," Fitz added, trying to easing him.

Fitz was leaning over the computers inside the upstairs room of the Fit n Foot. Mr. Shultz stood behind the kids with his shoulders slumped, frowning.

"Do you kids even know how to work these computers?" Mr. Shultz asked.

Fitz burst out in chuckles.

"Do I know how to operate them? Does a level 15 fire elemental require a level 16 water defense attack?" Fitz giggled as he typed rapidly at the keyboard.

In mere seconds, Fitz had all four cameras in the store up on four divided screens on Mr. Shultz's computer.

"As you can see, Fitz is an expert at this type of stuff Mr. Shultz," Donell exclaimed.

Camera 1 was directly above the counter of the store. This showed the whole area of the store except for those who are behind the counter and the women's shoe section that is beside the counter.

Camera 2 was a camera on the far wall that showed the counter and the women's section of the shoe department.

Camera 3 displayed the hallway in the backroom storage area, the shelves where the shoeboxes were stacked and the back door.

Camera 4 was on the outside of the building and showed nothing but blackness from the recent administration of grape bubble gum on the lens, which was discovered by Peg.

Fitz's fingers flew over the keyboard. He was very fast and before Mr. Shultz could say another word, Fitz had brought up what all of the cameras recorded for the morning after the store was opened.

"Now watch this," Fitz remarked.

He connected his personal laptop with Mr. Shultz's computer with a series of wires. His screen showed his email, an adventure game he is playing, and a funny video of a ferret doing a hula dance routine.

Fitz pointed to the screens that he was concerned with at the moment—the screens concerning the cameras, not the dancing ferret.

"There is verification that you received Mystic Bradley's shoes Mr. Shultz," Fitz said.

He was looking at Camera 1 and it showed that the time was 8:15 a.m. It showed a black and white version of Mr. Shultz accepting a package at the door of the store.

"There. Do you see? There are the shoes. I put them on the center display case," Mr. Shultz remarked.

He pointed nervously at the computer screen.

"I can see the stripe and everything. Wow! The shoes that Mystic Bradley used to win game 7! Totally cool," Donell said, leaning over Fitz's shoulder looking at the screen.

Fitz was fast forwarding through the time in the camera so he could see the events. It made a high pitched winding sound and made the images move quickly, like they had been struck by lightning.

"According to the electronic records, approximately at 8:15 in the morning, Mr. Shultz received a package that had the shoes in them. At 8:17, he used Ed's shoe cleaner on them, and tied the laces. Then at 8:19 he placed them on the glass center display case before his employees arrived. But what is that tag you are putting on them around 8:20?" Fitz asked Mr. Shultz.

"Oh. Yes. You see!? That is a security tag. I have them on all of my shoes so if anyone tries to walk out of the store a noisy alarm will go off," Mr. Shultz said.

"Very interesting, so the thief could not have possibly gone out the front door with them. That narrows the suspects down to those that have access to the back door," Fitz said, typing and fast forwarding the events.

"None of my employees can go out the back without me giving them the key. Today, I just sent Marcus out. He emptied the trash and also the shoe recycling bin before I sent them all home," Mr. Shultz said.

"Aha! That narrows it down to one then. His name starts with a Marcus, and it ends with a Marcus," Donell replied, grinding his teeth.

"That is most probable," Fitz said.

He watched the screens in front of him, continuing to scan through both Camera 1 and Camera 2.

"And now two employees arrive at 8:30 a.m.," said Fitz and wheeled around, pointing to Camera 1 which showed a taller girl entering the store. Following at her heels was a smaller boy about the same age as Donell and Fitz.

The Private Eye Five

"And there they are. The two workers. That is Lee. He goes to our school. But who is the older girl?" Donell asked Mr. Shultz.

"Yes. Who indeed?" Fitz wondered in a dreamy voice.

"She's a student at Towson High. Her name is Shanna. She works for me part-time now. She is an excellent worker. And then there is...Marcus." Mr. Shultz exclaimed and shook his head.

They all looked at the computer.

On Camera 1, at 8:45, closest to the store counter, the kids watched Marcus strolling in to the store chewing gum and blowing big sticky bubbles. He was talking loudly to his friends in the street and hanging beside the door. When he finally entered, he was checking his phone and laughing to himself.

"It is 8:45. Marcus is late," Mr. Shultz sighed.

"There he is. There is that slimy thief," Donell said.

"We can't verify that yet Donell," Fitz stated.

"It would be just like him to ruin my chance at seeing Mystic and getting him to sign my basketball," Donell leaned closer to the screen. He gripped his basketball tightly in his hands.

"Marcus was in my sight the whole time, and I was up front all morning. Look," Mr. Shultz exclaimed.

He pointed to the screen of Camera 2 on the computer.

Camera 2 showed Mr. Shultz working at the counter, sweating and muttering. He was filling out paperwork. It was easy to see in the screen that he was anxious to get the Mystic Bradley event underway. Around the store are big paper rolls, a table for Mystic to sign autographs on, and many balloons which Lee and Marcus were blowing up to get ready for the event.

Shanna was directing Lee.

Fitz fast forwarded and it showed that Mr. Shultz was indeed in the front of the store the whole time. Both cameras also showed Shanna and Lee working tirelessly while Marcus drifted around the store.

As time sped on, both cameras in the front of the store, Fitz, Donell, and Mr. Shultz noticed that Lee was putting up a big banner to introduce the event. Meanwhile, Shanna was taking care of customers and directing Lee while he was up on a step ladder. She was also helping place the balloons and small banners that she made with magic markers.

"Shanna certainly is a diligent worker," Fitz said.

He zoomed in on her. He watched her toss her long hair back while kneeling down and measuring a customer for the right shoe size.

Donell cleared his throat and waved his hand in front of Fitz's face.

"Hey Fitz, are you okay, man? Earth to Fitz," Donell blurted.

"Yes. I am Donell. I was just…umm, gathering information," Fitz stammered.

Donell rolled his eyes and laughed.

"Of course you were, my man," Donell said and patted Fitz on the shoulder.

Donell examined Camera 1, which gave the best view of Marcus.

"Look at Marcus. All this time while they both are working, he is blowing bubbles, walking around, tossing balloons in the air and looking on his phone." Donell said with gritted teeth.

Both cameras showed Shanna racing back and forth from the counter to the back room. Lee was struggling with the banner and Marcus was taking many breaks.

"Yes. Marcus can be a challenge. Today I was so busy I didn't have time to correct him," Mr. Shultz remarked.

"Okay. So we see what they all are doing. Can you zoom in on the shoes Fitz? At some point somebody grabbed them and replaced them," Donell instructed, leaning in.

Fitz's fingers fly on the keyboard. He zoomed in on the shoes, but the closer he got, the more blurry the details became.

"Tic Tik Tak Tak Tik Tik Tik Tak Takka Tak", the keyboard clamored.

"Sorry, Donell. The closer I get the more the composition breaks down. What a can do is add a Halo program which will indicate any sudden change in the shoe image. Let me get on my laptop and find one," Fitz added emphatically.

"Come on, Fitz. No fancy programs, man. Just keep your eye on the shoes. Then we will see Marcus when he snatches them. It is simple. No fast forwarding either," Donell pleaded.

"I understand what you are saying Donell. But with a Halo program I can scan everything all at once. The program will tell me the exact time they were stolen. That way I can look at all the cameras at one time," he stammered.

Fitz tried desperately to explain to Donell his methods, but Donell just shook his head.

"Look, Fitz. You are good with computers, but all you have to do is watch the shoes this time, using your eyeballs," Donell said, putting a hand on Fitz's shoulder.

"I'll try, Donell," Fitz replied unenthusiastically and quietly.

"Good. While you do that, I'm hitting the block. I know where Marcus likes to hang out and play basketball with the older kids. If I'm lucky I can catch him with the shoes and get back in time," Donell told him.

"Be careful, Donell. Taking Peg would be a wise choice. A wiser choice would be to arm yourself with an impenetrable force field or at least a battle axe," Fitz

informed him.

"I don't have that, but thanks. I just want to get close

enough to see what's up and maybe snap a picture with my

phone," Donell said and started walking out.

"Hey Fitz, don't fall in love while I'm gone," Donell

added, pointing at Shanna on the screen.

On the screen, Shanna was racing to the back room with a

shoebox. Fitz muttered something nervously but Donell

didn't hear him.

Donell leapt down the steps, nodded to Peg and Lily and

walked quickly out the door. He did not want to hear about

Lily's magic tricks or the weird places Peg was looking for

the shoes. He had looked forward to this day for a month

and it seemed like it was crashing down all around him—

and his friends were just joking around. He could only trust

himself, he thought.

Donell headed to the court, dribbling his basketball. There were many in conversation about the events that happened, and Donell kept a trained ear out for any important news.

An old lady said that she saw a man and his dog running out of the store with the shoes in his mouth. Two teens said Mr. Shultz stole them himself. Others said that Marcus had something to do with it and some even hinted that Mystic Bradley came in disguise and replaced the sneakers because he was rumored to be traded to another city.

"Why the long face, Donell? You look like someone stole your lunch money," a voice called out.

Donell turned to see a short girl in a plaid skirt and brown sweater.

"Hey Marissa. I'm just chilling. What's with the badge?" Donell asked.

He pointed to the sewn patch around Marissa's neckline.

"This is my rank, Donell. I joined a group called Strong Women's Association of Math Prowess. I am a cadet. We are a group that encourages women and girls to pursue careers in math. We go on field trips to science fairs, math battles, and bake cookies shaped like algebra signs. Would you like to buy a box of integers?" She asked Donnell, holding out a box.

Donell laughed, patting his tummy.

"No, thank you. I just had some mixed fractions for breakfast," Donell chided her, and tossed his basketball in the air nonchalantly, frowning.

"Strong Women's Association of Math Prowess? Swamp? You are aware that is what it spells right?" Donell tells Marissa, pointing toward her patch.

"S...W...A...M...P...? I guess that is right. Oh well," Marissa laughed.

Donell chuckled but looked away. He was distracted despite Marissa being very cheerful.

"There is something wrong with you today, Donell," Marissa pointed out and waved her finger.

"You wouldn't understand. Basically, I am trying to catch a thief and my friends aren't taking it seriously. Sometimes all they want to do is joke around," he told her.

"You don't think I get that? Donell, I am the only girl in my grade that has a fully workable college portfolio already. I understand you perfectly! They think that I act too serious and I think that they don't act serious enough," Marissa told him.

"That's right! Maybe you can help me then," Donell said to her.

"Sure Donell. I can try," Marissa replied enthusiastically.

"Great. Thanks Marissa. With your help we'll catch Marcus," Donell said.

"Marcus Jones? He once pulled the chair out from under me and I fell on the floor. Okay. Tell me the case," she said.

Donell told Marissa all he knew, while Fitz and Mr. Shultz were still upstairs looking at the cameras and Peg and Lily were looking around the store for clues.

"I have heard of Shanna. She is an eleventh grader and involved in a lot of clubs," Marissa remarked.

"According to Fitz she is also a princess that floats in the clouds," laughed Donell.

Marissa laughed too.

"He's being a lover boy, eh?" She playfully asked.

When Donell only rolled his eyes, Marissa continued, getting down to business.

"I can find out more about her by making a few calls. I know everyone in the groups she is a part of. I can say I might be doing a paper on her. I am a part-time writer for our school newspaper anyway, you know," Marissa told Donell.

"And I can also get information about Lee," Marissa added after seeing Donell's blank expression.

"I think Marcus stole the shoes, Marissa. I can't see why we should put Lee and Shanna in this," Donell wondered.

"Because Donell, even if Marcus did it, that doesn't mean anything. Are they working with him? Did they know about the crime beforehand? They are still suspects," Marissa corrected.

"Okay. So what do we do then?" Marcus questioned.

"I can ask around and see if there is anything funny going on. If there is something odd about Lee or Shanna, I will find out about it. Meanwhile, you can get dirt on Marcus and we can report back to the shoe store in an hour," Marissa instructed.

"Wow. Okay, Marissa. I guess we can try. Hey, where did you learn about solving crimes?" Marcus asked.

"Don't you ever watch detective shows, Marcus? It never is the one that you suspect. It is always either the butler, or the old grandmother, or the mailman," Marissa told him firmly.

Donell giggled despite not agreeing completely with Marissa.

"Okay. We meet back in an hour. Marcus likes to watch the older kids play basketball at the outdoor courts. I bet you he would love to show off those shoes he stole," Donell told her.

"Be careful, Donell," Marissa told him before she dashed off, already running through names in her phone.

"I will because today, I don't think the mailman did it," Donell said and headed down the street.

He was worried too but tried to remain calm. There were a lot of older kids who played at that court.

Baffling Balloons, Banners, and Boxes

Chapter 4

"I'll get you," Mr. Shultz barked.

He had Fitz's headset on and his laptop. He shook his fist at the screen.

Mr. Shultz was playing a video game that Fitz had showed him. Fitz did so because Mr. Shultz had been looking over his shoulder and worrying too much. This way, Mr. Shultz could concentrate on surviving the second class hydra dragon while Fitz looked over the cameras in the store without being disturbed.

In the game, Mr. Shultz's character wore a hood and was armed with a staff. He was in a cave, and the dragon was snoring and sleeping in the water. The dragon's belly rose up as it breathed heavily. Every time it snored, bats fluttered out of the corners of the cave, squeaking.

"What do I do now?" Mr. Shultz begged Fitz.

"Cross the river of many woes and reclaim the golden chest," Fitz responded.

"The water looks too cold," Mr. Shultz complained.

Fitz was still scanning through the events, looking for anything suspicious.

He looked at the two screens of the camera footage from that morning. He used the mouse to draw a bright blue circle around the shoes. The circle was part of a computer program that would alert Fitz to any type of changes made to the targeted object. The shoes in the center were the target. The very moment the shoes were swiped, Fitz's program would tell him about it by changing color.

The blue circle would flash red, and Fitz would know exactly what time the shoes were replaced, the one who stole them, and the thief's tricky methods.

Meanwhile, the shoe store owner was focused on escaping the creepy cave in his video game.

Fitz studied the cameras. His fingers flew over the keys and navigated the mouse.

Both cameras showed the older, more responsible and very pretty Shanna, ordering Lee as he was trying to hang the big banner. She was also taking care of the first customers that came in the store while Marcus strolled around and tried to look busy.

Every time Shanna looked up at the camera, Fitz giggled to himself. Then he shook it off quickly, realizing that Donell needed him.

"Be strong, Fitz. This is no time for romance and revelry. Nay! The hoary, cold hand of justice must first come to the perpetrator," Fitz mumbled to himself.

"What's that?" Mr. Shultz looked back and enquired, removing his headphones.

"Nothing, Mr. Shultz," Fitz stammered.

Fitz refocused his attention on the screen.

He observed on the camera that Marcus started the day refusing to work. It was adding stress to Shanna. She was already looking nervous and pacing as much as Mr. Shultz. Marcus was pretending to sweep the rug but he was really looking at his phone. Fitz zoomed in to the phone.

It was blurry but he saw it was a basketball game on BlurbTube, the same video website with the dancing ferret.

"Interesting," Fitz said to himself, making a mental note.

Fitz watched the screen as Shanna helped some other customers try on shoes. She raced to the backroom.

"Poor damsel, Marcus is putting her in frequent distress," Fitz whispered to himself.

Meanwhile, Mr. Shultz was walking around the water's edge in the video game. The bats were squeaking at him and diving in his hair.

"Ouch," he yelped and jumped in his seat like they are attacking him in real life.

But, Fitz's mind took on all the screens at once. His eyes darted quickly to and fro, absorbing information and events.

On Camera 1, Fitz observed Lee balancing on a ladder trying to put up the banner for the event. Marcus was standing near the door and walking near the window frequently whenever he heard loud car speakers, a dog bark, or somebodies' voice he recognized.

Suddenly Fitz was interrupted from his thoughts by Mr. Shultz's gravelly plea.

"Fitz. Young man! How do I drive this thing?" Mr. Shultz cried out.

In the video game, Mr. Shultz's character was in a boat. He was rowing in circles. Around and around he went, swirling through the river of Many Woes.

"You have to use both paddles Mr. Shultz, not just one," Fitz said without taking his eyes off the cameras.

"Oh," Mr. Shultz whined, but continued to play the game.

On Camera 1, Fitz observed that Marcus got close to the shoes many times in the morning hours. He would look at them pop bubbles and even put up his foot to measure his size 7s with Mystic Bradley's size 15s.

"Interesting, Marcus seems very curious about the shoes," Fitz muttered, more to himself than anyone else in the room.

Mr. Shultz was too distracted by the River of Many Woes to hear him.

"Help, I fell off the boat! And who is laughing at me in this headset?" Mr. Shultz cried out.

"They are your guild members, Mr. Shultz. You are in my internet gaming group," Fitz called out to him.

On the video game, Mr. Shultz's character was splashing through the river of Many Woes. Then another boat swung by and picked him up.

"Thank you young fellow," Mr. Shultz said to a fellow guild member through the headset.

There is a pause and then Mr. Shultz stood up and threw a tantrum. He stomped his feet and shook his fist at the laptop screen.

"I do not have the brains of a bird," he yelled into the microphone.

Someone in his guild had called him a bird brain. Mr. Shultz is not used to the type of trash talk that goes on in internet video games. How they could disrespect a reputable shoe store owner like that was shocking, he thought.

Fitz chuckled.

"They don't mean anything by it, Mr. Shultz. They just don't want you to wake the dragon up and ruin the quest. Once you cross the river, you have to borrow some dry pants and a tunic from a guild member using your 'beg and plead' buttons.

"Very well," Mr. Shultz said and sat back down.

On the video game, Mr. Shultz's character begged a warrior named Dennis2cool for extra clothes from his satchel.

Fitz smiled and continued to scan through the two cameras while Mr. Shultz hung his wet pants on a rock in the cave.

Fitz saw that on Camera 1, later in the morning, Lee managed to stretch a big paper banner to the other side of the wall, the wall closest to Camera 1. As Lee goes moved the banner around, it would sometimes block camera 1 entirely, much to Fitz's frustration.

However, when Camera 1 was blocked, Camera 2 was still clear, so he still had a sight on the shoes and what was happening with the three workers.

But as time sped by, since Fitz was seeing this in fast forward, Camera 2 was also getting blocked from time to time by floating balloons from the day's big event drift up toward the ceiling. Every time a balloon drifted, it blocked camera 2 until it blew away or someone moved it.

Fitz observes that around 11:25 a.m., Marcus was watching out the window, and not helping the other two. Shanna was busy with customers and Marcus didn't seem to care. He was falling asleep and still managing to blow bubbles with his gum. He nodded off many times standing up.

"Marcus seems to be watching from the window, or trying to. He must be excited for Mystic too," Fitz said to himself.

"Okay, I have dry clothes. I have the staff of whispers, whatever that is. Now what," Mr. Shultz asked Fitz, creeping over and shaking Fitz on the shoulder.

Fitz sighed. Some people just can't handle the common sense decision-making of today's video games, he thought.

"Okay. You are a sneaky class Mr. Shultz. That means that you have to be quiet and reclaim the golden chest from the dragon's treasure room. You have to be very quiet, Mr.

Shultz. If the dragon wakes up, a blast from its breath will turn you to solid gold," Fitz told him and wheeled around.

"What do I do? I'm scared," Mr. Shultz begged as he put one quivering hairy hand on Fitz's shoulder for support.

"You can do it, Mr. Fitz. You tell that dragon you will not go quietly into the night, good sir!" Fitz shouted, shaking a fist in the air.

Fitz saw that while he was trying to playfully inspire Mr. Shultz, the blue circle turned to flashing red.

"Whoa! I have to rewind this. I think we can solve this case, Mr. Shultz! Mr. Shultz?" Fitz turned.

The shoe store owner didn't hear Fitz. He was talking to his guild members on the headset and hunched over playing.

"Okay. I have a pair of dry pants at last and I am sneaking up to the dragon very quietly. Oops, I'm being careful not to step on any coins. They jangle and make noise," Mr. Fitz said to the headset.

Fitz laughed.

"Mr. Shultz is going to make a great gamer after all," he said to himself.

But back to the case, Fitz reminded himself, and rewinded the Cameras looking for the exact time the blue circle turned red.

What he saw shocked and disappointed him.

He doesn't see anything! Both Camera 1 and Camera 2

were blocked at the very moment the shoes were swiped!

"Donell is not going to like this," Fitz moaned and smacked his hand to his forehead.

They were hoping to find the thief, not a blacked-out camera.

While Fitz ran program after program to check if his systems were accurate, Lily and Peg were downstairs with a more hands-on approach to the case.

Lily was trying to think rationally and get her magic tricks out of her head. She wanted to prove that she was valuable to the case in a logical way.

Peg meanwhile was convinced that the shoes were hidden somewhere in the store. After she looked under the carpet and behind the posters, she grew even more desperate in her frantic search. She raced around Lily, searching like a happy puppy sniffing out a treat.

She looked in places that size 15 shoes couldn't possibly be, like behind balloons and inside of other shoes. When she was finished, she tossed the shoes on the ground and spun to another section. All around her there were shoes scattered all over the place. Peg didn't mean to be so messy, but just tended to get carried away.

Lily was sitting quietly on a stool, cross-legged, while Peg searched everywhere.

She looked in the trashcan behind the counter, spilling it out and bobbing her head.

"All of these wrappers must be a clue, Lily," Peg muttered while spreading the trash on the ground. She discovered two things—the name brand of the gum that Marcus likes and an empty carton of strawberry milk. The gum wrapper was Big Grape-Zillah and had a purple dinosaur made of fruity grapes.

"Let's try looking in the storage room in the back, Peg. But let's try not to scatter the shoes all around," Lily instructed her.

They went through a door into a dimly lit hallway. At the end of the hallway there was a bright yellow recycling bin with a hole cut at the top of it. It looked almost like the recycling bin around the back of the store where Lily did her trick, except smaller.

"There sure is a bunch of banana colored bins around this place," Peg remarked.

She put both hands around the bin and sniffed inside.

"Pewww! Smells like my older brother's room," Peg said and scrunched up her nose.

Lily looked inside too. The bin was empty. Around the side of the bin were the letters scribbled in magic marker:

"Recycled Shoes"

"No wonder it stinks, dude," Peg said.

"Yes. This is where our old sneakers go when we get new ones. Goodbye old sneakers. May you find peace in your new life," Lily waved inside the bin.

Peg cackled.

"What an odd place for a mirror, Peg. Look," Lily said to her.

Lily pointed to a scratched mirror on the wall above the shoe recycling bin.

The girls looked at their reflection in the mirror and made silly faces in it. Peg stuck her tongue out while Lily tugged on her ears and shut one eye like a pirate.

Then with roving eyes, Peg saw all the shoe boxes around her, stacked neatly and by sizes, on dusty shelves.

They laughed, and stroll towards the shelves where the shoeboxes sat.

"Wow! There are so many! How can we look through them all without making a mess?" Lily asks Peg.

She looked at Peg who just shrugged her knobby shoulders.

"Being orderly was never my thing, Lily," Peg laughed.

"But, we can handle this, Peg. Let us start with one shoe box at a time," Lily said to her.

To demonstrate, Lily went to the far shelf and picked up a box. The lack of weight surprised her.

"There must be a baby sneaker or maybe an angel's shoe in here. This box is light as air," Lily said to Peg.

Peg slid over to her and craned her head to look at the shoe box. Lily opened the lid of the box and gasps. What she was expecting were shoes, cardboard and some of that tissue paper that sits at the bottom of a shoebox.

What Lily saw were shoes, alright. They were her own shoes, on her own feet! Lily was looking at the ground, through the shoebox!

"This shoebox has had the bottom cut from it with scissors? Now that is really strange," Lily remarked, shaking her head.

Peg quickly grabbed the box and put her hand through it at the bottom.

"Look, Peg, those shoes are in here and I'm going to find them. It's time to do some climbing. Sorry Lily, I'll try to be neat," Peg remarked.

Peg threw the bottomless shoe box down and started climbing the shelves like a monkey.

She climbed quickly and was soon at the dusty top shelf. The shelf tottered back and forth, but Peg was light and nimble.

Lily glances at the shoe box with the bottom cut out of it. She picks it up and studies it closely. The more she sees it, the more she thinks of her magic book.

"Be serious Lily and think rationally," Lily scolded herself.

Lily placed the bottomless shoebox back on the shelf closest to the exit where she found it. She thought of many logical reasons why a shoe box would have the bottom cut out. One of them made the most sense.

"Marcus was probably fooling around with scissors. No big deal," she told herself.

But, she barely heard Peg who was looking in every shoebox for the shoes and singing music lyrics the whole time. Lily still felt the urgent need to look through her magic book.

"Unity in the community, unity in the community," Peg sang loudly.

From below, the tissue paper found in shoe boxes came floating down like bulky snowflakes. It rained on Lily who was lost in thought and talking quietly to herself. She didn't notice how much of a mess Peg was making up there while she was singing and searching.

Peg didn't know either. She thought she was just grooving to her music pounding in her ears and helping out her best friends in the entire world.

Chapter 5

Marissa, Mouse-O-Phobia and Mad Marcus

Marissa found a quiet place in the park to make the calls. As a math cadet for S.W.A.M.P., she already had her backpack with her. It was unzipped. She rummaged through it and found her sales notebook and a pen. She was talking on her phone and jotting down the information her sources provided her. She was writing very quickly and making side observations that she scribbled in different colored ink. As a reporter, she was used to writing fast.

It wasn't long until she filled up five pages each with

both Shanna and Lee's information. She closed her notebook with supreme satisfaction, and went over in her head what she wrote down. She thought, if I can memorize the information, then I can produce it even if somehow my notes get destroyed or we need the information in a hurry.

She was always thinking about the next step and planning ahead.

"I hope Donell will listen to me though. He seems very determined that Marcus acted alone," Marissa told herself.

Further down the street, Donell hunted Marcus down. He knew exactly where to look for him. It was at the outdoor basketball court where the older teens liked to hang out.

Donell didn't go there. He played basketball inside the Boys and Girls Community Center building. They always had nice new basketballs and shining glass backboards, and Teddy G sometimes played with them. Teddy G was always helpful, showing them tips on how to play the game better. He owned the place and kept it in good condition.

Donell strolled down the block listening to the angry traffic. The streets were bustling with people. Some were quiet and some were loud and noisy. All of them seemed to be in a rush to get to places. Donell usually wasn't like that. He liked to take in his surroundings.

On this day though, he was rushing, and had a good reason for it.

He got to a place where he could see the court through the chain link fence.

Everything about the outdoor courts was different, Donell observed.

He saw that the bleachers were leaning, there was trash blowing everywhere, and one basketball rim didn't have a net. The other had a chain net that hung off by a few rusted links.

He also saw the backboard had graffiti all over it and the concrete was cracked in a bunch of places.

"Man! Why can't they make this look better," Donell asked himself.

As he got closer, Donell noticed the older teens playing. Marcus was also in the game with them and having a hard time of it. He was an eighth grader playing against high school guys.

Donell rested his hands against the chain-link fence. He noticed Marcus was breathing heavy from the game. It surprised him to see that he was wearing a Mystic Bradley basketball jersey.

But Marcus couldn't pull off the moves of Mystic although he was trying real hard. He faked to one side and tried to dribble to the left, but the ball was stolen from him.

Donell had never really seen Marcus interact with teens who were older than him before this. He looked noticeably slower and smaller than all of them. The older kids also seemed to be teasing Marcus like Marcus torments Donell and his friends.

One teen dribbled by Marcus as he tried to steal the ball and laughed at him. Others joined in too. Donell could see from far away that it was embarrassing him. Some friends of Marcus's were watching him play but they all were silent, sitting apart from the group. They were also eighth graders and felt very uncomfortable next to ninth, tenth, eleventh and even twelfth graders.

Marcus smiled and wiped his hands on his pants but Donell could see he was trying hard to stay calm. He bragged loudly and talked confidently, but his actions on the court didn't back it up.

Those on the sidelines were cheering for everyone but Marcus. Further in the game, Marcus got his shot blocked by a bigger teen and cried foul. He held his back, wincing

in pain. He limped to the sideline, rubbing his back and his

shoulders.

"Hey! That is a foul," Marcus croaked.

"Foul, no way Marcus. You are just soft," An older teen in

a black tank top told him.

"I'm not soft. You are the one that is frozen yogurt,"

Marcus spouted back.

"Get off the court man. And take that jersey off. Mystic

Bradley wouldn't cry like a baby when he gets his shot

blocked," The older teen told him.

They chose someone to replace Marcus on the court and

commenced play.

"He would if he got hit like I got hit. Ouch, I think I popped

a disk in my back! Help," Marcus cried.

He shambled toward the bleachers, moving like an old

man, and sat beside his friends.

"Are you done Marcus?" One of his fellow eighth graders asked.

"Yes, for today. They are lucky I hurt myself. Did you see that foul? My back is on fire," Marcus whined, wincing as he sat down.

His friends shook their heads.

"You said you were going to show up those guys today Marcus," one of his friends reminded him.

"Hey, man. It's not my fault the guy plays like a bull that just stepped on a ketchup packet," Marcus cried out.

Donell crept closer to Marcus and the other eighth graders. To a seventh grader, it was like creeping toward a den of bears. But these bears looked defeated.

Donell watched while the eighth graders made weak excuses about why they couldn't hang out with Marcus the rest of the afternoon. They left him on the bleachers and Marcus continued to mouth excuses about why he is done playing.

Suddenly, it was just Marcus there all by himself and Donell watching him. In a flash, Marcus yanked off his Mystic Bradley jersey and threw it to the ground.

Then, Marcus seemed to sense Donell looking at him and turned to grin at him. Seeing Donell seemed to enliven Marcus.

"Hey four eyes! How are you? How are your nerd friends?" Marcus asked through the chain-link fence.

Marcus shambled to his feet and drifted lazily over until he stood close to Donell. He leaned against the chain-link fence and watched Donell through the links.

"Do you know about the stolen shoes Marcus?" Donell said, trying to be brave.

A wide, wicked grin spread over the face of Marcus. He blew a big purple bubble until it popped.

"Sure. I know all about them, four eyes. I bet you would love to know what I know. What's the matter? Did your big hero lose his widdle shoes?" Marcus taunted.

The Private Eye Five

"Don't worry, Marcus, me and my 'nerd friends', are on the case," Donell told him sternly and walked off. Even through a chain-link fence, Marcus could be scary.

Marcus leaned on the fence and laughed hysterically. He gripped the links of the chains and shook them. "Mystic Bradley is a chump! He can't play ball!" Marcus shouted.

When Donell was out of yelling range, Marcus turned around, swiped his dirty Mystic Bradley jersey and slowly shambled off the court.

Donell raced back to the shoe store. He was more convinced than ever that his first hunch was right and it was Marcus who took the shoes. Now he just had to catch him in the cameras. He wanted nothing more than to wipe that grape smirk off Marcus's face.

Marissa met Donell at the front of the Fit n Foot and could't wait to tell Donell about what she discovered about

Shanna and Lee. But in Donell's mind, there was only one suspect.

"His name begins with a Marcus, and ends with a Marcus," thought Donell.

"I'm glad you came back alive, Donell. Were there eighth graders?" She asks him, wide eyed.

"Yes, and some of them were older than that. I was in the mouth of the dragon," Donell told her.

But he was distracted with getting upstairs and incriminating Marcus. However, Marissa tugged on Donell's shirt insisting on giving him the information she had uncovered.

Marcus sighed. Marissa could be very forceful at times.

"Do you want to know what I found out?" Marissa asked.

"Marcus pretty much admitted that he stole the shoes, Marissa. I don't know what good it will do," Donell told her.

"Fine, Donell. It was the plan that we spilt up and gather information. You gathered yours and I gathered mine. I would think you would want to know what I did. Just like I want to know what you found out. It might help with the case. Don't you agree?" Marissa said, pointing and gesturing to Donell.

"Okay, okay, Marissa. Marcus told me that he knows about the shoes and that I would love to know what he knows," Donell told her.

"Oh. So he didn't exactly give you a confession of guilt. He just said he knows about them," Marissa said and made a mental note of it.

Donell smirked.

"The way he grinned at me was all the evidence I needed," Marcus told her.

"Donell grins like that when he is in a good mood. He probably grins like that on his birthday. I'm not saying you are wrong, but you can't let your personal feelings for him make you convict him without proof. On all the detective shows, they gather information and talk it out," Marissa said, perturbed that Donell was so anxious to get back in the shoe store.

"Sure, Marissa, now let's see if Fitz—" Donell started to say.

He was very anxious to get proof of Marcus because there was still a chance that Mystic could make an appearance. But Marissa blocked him from the doorway. She interrupted him and looked him squarely in the eyes.

"Now you can hear about my information and when you get upstairs, you can quickly use it if you need it. That is what detectives do. Plan, discuss, and then act," Marissa insisted, shaking her finger.

"Okay, okay. Tell me what you have, Marissa," Donell said, breathing a frustrated sigh.

"Very well," Marissa said and stood very still trying to remember the important information she gathered.

Donell threw up his hands and sat down on the curb in front of the shoe store. He knew Marissa and knew that it is a losing battle to ignore her. He might as well hear what she had to say, nod, and then race up the stairs.

Marissa sat down next to Marcus and unzipped her backpack.

"Time is of the essence so I took the liberty of writing down some of the more important information in red ink. Here is what I have," Marissa remarked.

"According to my main sources, Shanna takes all the college prep classes, has very good grades, and is the captain of the cheerleader squad, the debate team, and the cross country club. She also plays in ping pong tournaments in weekends and has won many regional championships in chess," Marissa told Donell.

To Donell, it was drifting in one ear, swimming through his brain, then out the other ear. He nodded though and gave Marissa a weak smile. Marissa nodded back and continued.

"I was very impressed with Shanna the more I learned about her. It was hard not to be impressed by her. She is intelligent, beautiful, and thinks a lot about her future preparing to go to college. In many ways I want to be just like her. She has one thing against her though. She has to have the most expensive name brand clothing. Yes, I understand looking nice, but there are sales you can find, and better, cheaper places..." Marissa trailed off.

Donell sighed.

"How did you find that out?" Donell asked her wearily.

"Because she told Connie Blake that she'll only be happy with a $500 dollar prom dress this year. Can you believe that?" Marissa spouted.

"Okay. Good information. That is good to know, now what about Lee?" Donell asked in a dreary voice.

"Lee is an eighth grader. He is always very shy and quiet and he also had excellent grades in class. He was on the honor roll every semester last year. He enjoys writing romantic poetry and BMX biking," Marissa told him.

Donell shrugged. He felt like he was watching one of those dating television shows, not listening to evidence in a crime. Marissa ignored Donell's tired gestures. "Lee goes to construction sites and practices his biking. He jumps ramps, does flips, and has been in a few races. He won a BMX championship in Dundalk last spring," she told him, reading from her notes.

"He also helps mow his grandmother's lawn on the weekends," Marissa told Donell.

Donell sarcastically thought, Great! But what does that have to do with the missing shoes?

Marissa scanned through her notebook. She followed the words with her eyes.

"Oh yes! This is a good one! He is always the kid that seems to fall in love quickly. He spent a lot of time making homemade hearts for Valentine's Day and handing them out to all of the girls. Oh. That is nice," Marissa said and tilted her head forward playfully.

"So he is a lover boy," Donell said in a droning voice, using Marissa's expression for Fitz earlier.

Donell stood up and yawned.

"Great, Marissa. Now if there isn't anything else…" Donell told her, balancing from one foot to the next.

"I have one last thing in red, Donell. It was at the beginning of the school year. There was an incident he once had in a science class where he tried to jump out of the first story window during a lab," Marissa replied, standing up and looking at Donell with her arms crossed.

"Jump out the window? Why would he do that?" Donell asked.

"Because someone let a little white mouse out of the cage and he has an unbelievably strong fear of them," Marissa told him and walked toward the shoe store.

She turned back to Donell and held up both hands like a mouse.

"Mouse-o-phobia! Squeak, squeak," she said to Donell in a playful tone.

She went in to the shoe store, leaving Donell standing by the curb and shaking his head.

He gripped his basketball. Maybe recruiting someone like Marissa wasn't such a great idea after all, he thought. He shrugged and hurried into the shoe store. He was ready to catch the true thief even if his friends weren't.

Chapter 6

The Gang Loses their Cool

Donell was more certain than ever that Marcus had something to do with the crime. He knew, as he charged into the shoe store, that Fitz was going to have video proof of it.

"Let's catch us a crook. Maybe I can see Mystic after all," Donell shouted.

"And that his charity receives the money," Marissa reminded him.

"Oh yeah, I almost forgot about that," Donell said and slapped his head.

How could I forget about the charity to educate kids like us, he thought to himself?

Donell and Marissa glanced around the store and saw that the place was a mess.

"What is going on here?" Marissa asked Donell.

"Three words Peg and Lily," Donell exclaimed.

They rushed to the backroom. Lily's magic bag of tricks was splayed out on the floor. She was reading something vigorously. Peg was up on the top shelf. Dust clouds and shoe tissue paper was raining down on them.

"Come on guys! This is it! I know you probably want to do anything but help, but you are tearing up the store!" Donell cried out.

Lily stopped reading her page and looked up.

Peg smiled down at Donell. There was a smudge of dirt under her nose.

"Hey dude. I just thought I would find the shoes here," she called down from above.

"Didn't Mr. Shultz tell us he checked everywhere in the store Peg?" Donell said.

"I don't remember that, but I can tell you now that the shoes aren't here. Lily thinks they disappeared. She's right I think," Peg said.

"No. I'm not right. I'm sorry Donell. I wanted to help," Lily blurted and stood up, shoving her book into her bag.

"How, Lily? By watching Peg wreck the place?! By saying that it is magic? I don't think so, Lily. Look, I'm going upstairs. Fitz is helping me and soon we will have Marcus," Donell told her.

He left them feeling very disappointed. He wished his friends would take something seriously.

Lily put her head down.

"Hey, Lily," Marissa said to her and waved.

"Hey, Marissa," Lily said quietly.

"Hey, Marissa," Peg called from up in her perch.

"Hey, Peg. Are you going to get down from there?" Marissa asked.

"Sure, dude. Let me clean this mess up first," Peg called out.

Lily walked out of the backroom with her head down. She tossed her magic bag in the trash can then plopped down on a stool, waiting for the other two.

"No more magic," she mumbled sadly.

In the back, there was a loud crash and Peg yelped.

"I'm okay. I broke my fall on Marissa!" Peg shouted.

"Oww. Peg, get off me!" Marissa said in a high pitched squeal.

Donell walked up the steps slowly. He didn't want to lose patience with his friends. He was upset though. He went out of his way to see Peg's skateboard trick and then she wrecked the shoe store. Then Lily watched her do it while playing with her magic, he thought.

When he got up the steps, he saw more that upset him. Instead of seeing Fitz at the computer, he was leaning over and helping Mr. Shultz get past the dragon in the game.

"Give him sleeping powder. No! That's sneezing powder," Fitz instructed Mr. Shultz.

"That will make the dragon sick, won't it?" Mr. Shultz looked over at Fitz.

"No. That will wake him. Oh no, Mr. Shultz. Get out of there! Don't tip toe. Run! Quick," Fitz yelled.

"I'm scared, young man. This is my first dragon," Mr. Shultz moaned.

"Hey, guys. I hope you have some good news for me," Donell said.

Mr. Shultz and Fitz both turned.

"Yes. I made it to sneaky class level 2 and I have the golden flute of time, young man," Mr. Shultz proudly boasted to Donell.

"Hey, Donell. I was just showing him this game while my programs are running last minute checks," Fitz replies.

"What did you find, my man? Let me hear some good news," Donell asked him, ignoring the game.

"Umm… okay. The good news is that I know the exact time when the sneakers were stolen. Here. Look." Fitz exclaimed while gesturing toward the computer.

Fitz showed him the camera and the blue circle turning to red.

"Okay. What is that?" Donell asked.

"It is a program that is designed to read changes. The time when the thief stole the shoes was 11:36 a.m.," Fitz stated.

"Yeah, but why are the cameras blocked out?" Donell asked impatiently.

"That is the problem, Donell. The exact time the sneakers were stolen, both Camera 1 and Camera 2 were blocked out. Camera 1 was blocked out by a paper banner. Camera 2 was blocked out by balloons Shanna placed minutes before to decorate the store," Fitz told him.

"What? Are you saying that we can't see Marcus stealing the shoes?" Donell questioned loudly.

"Before the camera was blocked out, Marcus was against the far wall falling asleep, so it would be physically improbable for him to take them. That may rule him out," Fitz informed.

"Then that means one thing, Fitz. Your computer program is messing up, man. It blocked out the cameras and you were busy playing a game and you didn't notice," Donell replied, raising his voice.

"No, Donell! I ran a bug check. I cleaned everything. I am telling you that the computer is functioning fine. I checked it and double checked it. Believe me, Donell," Fitz stammered.

"Lily is playing with magic. Peg is wrecking the store. You are up here helping Mr. Shultz slay a dragon…"

"Actually recover a golden chest from a second class hydra dragon. It is more about stealth," Mr. Shultz corrected.

"I want to believe you, Fitz, but it just looks like you are all playing around," Donell said, letting his temper flare.

"Nobody wants to capture Marcus more than me! I am just telling you what I see on the camera. You have to believe me," Fitz blurted.

They started to argue when Mr. Shultz stood and removed his headphones. He stepped in between the two kids who were pointing at each other and started to yell over their voices. He addressed Donell.

"Now listen, young man. Your friend has been scurrying around trying to figure out what is on the cameras. I saw him. I recommend him any day with my technology. He showed me how to cross the river, get a dry pair of pants, and gave me confidence to grab the golden chest and avoid those bats," Mr. Shultz responded with a booming voice.

"While the programs were running, I showed him some tricks in the game. I am not fooling around. There has to be a reasonable explanation to this. I know there is," Fitz pleaded

"Your friends are very smart. All of them. Don't leave them when they want to help you out," Mr. Shultz instructed.

Donell sighed.

"Okay. Let's get the others up here. Let's see what we have for clues," Donell said with his head down.

"That's the spirit. I'll go and get them and while I'm at it, I'll buy some ice cream sandwiches from the Burp-A-Lot," Mr. Shultz said happily.

"What about the game, Mr. Shultz?" Fitz asked.

"My guild abandoned me and the dragon turned me to gold anyway, my young friend," Mr. Shultz said.

When Mr. Shultz went downstairs, he was surprised by the state of his shoe store. There were shoes everywhere. Mr. Shultz shook his bald head.

Marissa was trying to clean up.

"I'm sorry, Mr. Shultz," Lily told him.

"Yes, sorry sir," Peg came out of the back trailing dust and shoe tissue paper on her shoes.

"It's okay. You kids are trying to help by solving a crime. Here. Your friends need you upstairs. I'll straighten the place up," Mr. Shultz said.

"Thanks mister shoe man. You are awesome," Peg cackled.

She bounded up the steps after grabbing her skateboard. Lily weakly smiled at Mr. Shultz and started to head upstairs.

"Now why would anyone throw this away?" Mr. Shultz called out after her.

He held up Lily's bag of magic tricks from out of the trashcan.

Lily turned, frowned, and looked down at the ground.

"Here, young lady. This belongs to you I believe. You must have accidentally thrown it away," Mr. Shultz handed it to her with a warm smile.

"Thanks," Lily said quietly and took the bag.

She walked slowly up the steps.

Marissa lingered behind with Mr. Shultz. They both looked around at the mess in the store and decided the Burp-A-Lot was the place to go first.

Lily and Peg could hear the bickering and arguing between the two close friends upstairs as they ascend the steps. Mr. Shultz was not there to separate them. Upstairs, Donell was pacing back and forth while Fitz sat, wheeled around in the chair trying to prove his point.

"So you mean to tell me that those sneakers just vanished?" Donell asked Fitz.

"Not vanished. The cameras were blocked. It was like the gum on the lens trick," Fitz said.

"But you are saying Marcus couldn't have taken them," Donell stated in a loud voice.

"I'm saying he was falling asleep at the window, Donell. The only one that could have possibly taken them, and that it hurts my heart to say, was the damsel, Shanna," Fitz concluded.

"Shanna? Come on Fitz, I saw Marcus. He was wearing a Mystics basketball jersey and he smiled at me. He knew something," Donell exclaimed.

"Shanna was helping a customer three meters from the shoes. And she was spotted on Camera 3 walking quickly to the back room shortly after they were stolen. Look, Donell. Seconds after the shoes are stolen this is what transpires in the back room. Just look," Fitz urged.

Lily, Peg, Donell and Fitz gather around the computer. The time on the camera, according to Fitz, is ten seconds after his programs say that the shoes were stolen.

They watch Shanna. She has a shoebox and is heading for the back.

"She is moving fast," Peg exclaimed.

"Well she has two customers waiting for her, so that is to be expected," Fitz remarked.

"Keep watching. There is something odd about her behavior," Fitz added.

Lily watched Shanna stride to the back room. She was carrying the shoebox down the same hall where her and Peg were moments ago. Lily recognized the hall and the shoe recycling bin.

She watched on Camera 3 as Shanna stopped at the recycling shoe bin and placed the box of sneakers down on the lid.

"Wow! Maybe she puts the stolen shoes in the recycling bin then comes back for them later," Donell, jumped up and pointed at the screen.

But as they watched, Shanna just checked herself in the mirror, smoothing back her long dark hair. She then picked up the shoe box and placed it on the bottom shelf, all the way to the end, near the back door.

"Nope," Donell declared with disgust.

"I didn't go into the backroom yet, but if Shanna took the shoes when both cameras were blocked, shoved them in the shoebox and set them on a shelf in the backroom, the shoes could still be there! Did anyone check?" Fitz asked enthusiastically, not knowing that Peg and Lilly had already searched every shoe box.

"Yeah, man. That was the first box me and Lily checked. I checked them all. I tore that place to pieces, dude," Peg sadly muttered.

Donell hung his head and slumped his shoulders. It seemed to be his last hope.

All of the kids hung their heads. If Shanna put the stolen shoes in the backroom, then Peg and Lily would have discovered them already.

The kids were all silent for a minute. Then Donell, in a defeated voice, uttered.

"Fitz. Man, you must have made a mistake. Your programs must be wrong," Donell told him.

That led to the kids bickering back and forth again. Fitz talked about the technical programs he ran, the de-bugging ones to check to see if his initial programs were correct. Donell argued back and told Fitz that he should have just watched one camera at a time.

Then Peg came to Donell's defense and told Fitz that there was nothing in the shoe boxes.

And all this put Lily in deep thought. She thought about the events that had transpired. One moment the shoes were there and the next moment, they vanished. She remembered Dices' comforting words, telling her that she would be valuable to the group. Suddenly the answer appeared to her.

It stuck out like a rabbit popping out of a hat!

"Wait a minute! Magic!" Lily shouted over them all.

The kids stopped bickering. Donell looked at Lily and rolled his eyes. Fitz did the same.

"Come on, Lily, are you talking about that again?" Donell said, becoming more and more frustrated with her.

"The bathroom is the place where Shanna put the shoebox on the shelf, Peg! Don't you remember what we found there?" Lily asked her excitedly.

Peg thought about it for a second, scratching her shaggy hair. Then with equal enthusiasm she shouted.

"Wait here, dudes. I'll go get it!"

Peg raced down and then was back up in seconds. She wasn't even panting when she returned. Peg was used to skateboarding all day so a trip up and down the steps was nothing to her. She gave the box to Lily and grinned.

"What is this about, Lily? Is this another one of your magic tricks?" Donell said, and chuckles.

Fitz even laughed at Lily. Lily ignored them and pointed to Camera 3 on the computer screen and the shoebox in her hand.

"This was in the place where Shanna put the shoebox down. Look," Lily said to them all.

She showed the kids the shoebox with the bottom cut out of it.

"So? What does that mean Lily?" Donell asked.

"It means that maybe Shanna used magic to steal the shoes," Lily said with confidence and laid the shoebox next to Fitz to examine it.

Chapter 7

Magic Shoes and Peg on the Hunt

Donell ccouldn't help but feel exhausted with his friends. He wanted to trust them but Lily's magic was discouraging him. Suddenly he wanted to go home and curl up in his bed.

"Lily. Thanks for trying to help me with the case, but I think I'll just head back home. You too Fitz, thanks for your help," Donell told them.

He grabbed his basketball from the corner and headed for the steps. But Fitz cut him off.

"It would be wise to hear her out Donell. I have researched magic and it is all about misdirection and fooling the eye," Fitz said.

Donell turned, feeling all of the frustration of the day.

"No. It is all about Lily and her latest hobby, Fitz," Donell told him.

"Hey, dude. Chill. Listen to her, man! Lily has been trying to help you. She even threw her magic tricks in the trash so she wouldn't be distracted," Peg blurted.

At that point, Donell stopped. He knew that when Lily started drawing, painting, practicing magic, or anything else, she threw everything she had into it. Hearing that Lily threw her magic book away to help him in the case made him stop and realize that his friends were more important than solving a mystery or getting an autograph.

"You did that, Lily?" Donell asked.

Lily nodded silently and looked away.

Just then, Mr. Shultz came back with Marissa. They had a bag full of cold, delicious goodness.

"I thought you smart detectives could all use an ice cream sandwich," Mr. Shultz shouted out jubilantly.

"Alright!" Peg pumped her fist in the air.

"That would be a most welcome and delicious payment for our services," Fitz agreed.

"Oh Fitz," Marissa laughed.

She nibbled on her sandwich careful not to spill anything on her sweater.

Hearing about Lily's effort and eating the ice cream encouraged Donell. Before, he had been ready to give up. But now he started seeing clearly. They had all been trying to help him and they all had qualities that make them special to him. That is why they were his friends in the first place.

After gathering around and disposing of the wrappers and getting that wonderful grainy chocolate on their fingertips and getting to the cold creamy middle, he spoke to them.

"Hey guys. Thanks for helping me with this case. I'm sorry, Fitz, for not trusting you. And Lily, I know that when you have a hobby you get really excited. I was excited about seeing Mystic Bradley, so I get it. Sorry for being selfish, guys," Donell said.

"Hey. We can still solve this thing," Lily told him between bites of her ice cream.

"That's right," Peg yelled.

"Okay, Lily. I want to hear this. I want you to make me a believer in magic," Donell laughed, but good-naturedly.

"Sure Donell, but before I go, why don't we review what we know first. I think magic will fill in the gaps," Lily told the group.

"Yes! Like real detectives. That is a great idea! I think because I thought of it first," Marissa said, giggling.

"Delightful," said Mr. Schultz with a mouthful of gooey ice cream sandwich in his cheeks.

"That is cool. So what do we know?" Donell questioned. He balled up his wrapper and tossed it in the trash.

Everyone was suddenly unsure of themselves. They had never been on a team trying to solve a crime. They were just kids and expected to just play some video games or watch a movie—not catch a thief. When no one answered, Donell started in, which began the first case discussion among many to follow.

"Okay. We know that the exact time the shoes were stolen and replaced with a different pair, both Camera 1 and Camera 2 were blocked off. Right, Fitz?" Donell motioned to Fitz.

"I don't know, Donell. It is like you said, I could have made a mistake with..." Fitz started to mutter.

"Let me stop you right there, Fitz. I trust you, man. You are a computer genius! Tell us what you know Ranger of the Wild Realms," Donell said and slapped Fitz on the shoulder.

Fitz smiled and looked away. Then he nodded to his friends who were all leaning in to hear him. Fitz wiped his mouth and cleared his throat.

"At exactly 11:36 a.m. the shoes were stolen. What was transpiring at the moment was Marcus was on the far wall, falling asleep. My guess is that he is also a big Mystic Bradley fan and was watching for his arrival. He was twelve meters from the shoes and looking out the window."

"Also, Lee was beside the register upon a step ladder adjusting the big paper banner. They could not have possibly taken the shoes," Fitz told them.

"Unless they moved at the speed of light," suggested Lily.

"Yes, unless they move at 299,792,458 meters per second," Fitz chuckled.

"Which leaves Shanna?" Marissa asked.

"She was the closest. Three meters away," Fitz said.

"Why can't we blame any customers?" Peg questioned.

"It couldn't have been a customer because there was a security tag on the shoes. If anyone left with them out the front door, a noisy alarm would have gone off," Donell informed her.

"It's true. I put one on them this morning," Mr. Shultz added.

"Does it sound like this? BEEP BEEP BEEP!" Peg shouted in the ear of Marissa who turned away and squealed!

"So that means that the shoes could have only been taken by Shanna," Marissa said after recovering from Peg's loud attack.

"Let's keep on going before making accusations. What else do we know?" Donell asked.

Fitz continued.

"We know that Camera 3, shortly after the shoes were stolen, shows Shanna carrying a shoe box. She then stops at the shoe recycling bin, and sets the box down on the lid."

"Yeah. And the bin is empty, but still smells like rotten potatoes," Peg piped up.

"It's true. We checked," laughed Lily.

"Okay. So now after Shanna sets the shoebox down, she looks in the mirror. After that, she picks it back up and moves the shoebox to the bottom shelf. That is where Lily and Peg discovered the shoe box with the bottom cut out from it," Donell exclaimed.

"What else do we know?" Marissa asked, really enjoying the exchange of information? She planned it to be like this.

"I think we know that the shoes are not in the store. This young lady saw to it that every corner of my store was turned upside down," Mr. Shultz said and ruffled Pegs hair.

"I ripped the place to shreds, dude," Peg said calmly, with pride.

"Alright, Lily. I am stumped. Fill in the gaps. Work your magic," Donell requested in between the last bite of his ice cream sandwich.

Lily soaked up the attention. Before then she felt like a nuisance, but now she saw why she was a part of the team. She thought about what she was going to say, but first, it was important that she demonstrated how the human eye could be fooled. How better to do it than with a magic trick, she thought?

Her coin magic trick!

She performed the trick, amazing her friends. Then, they were ready for the explanation.

"Like Fitz said, magic is about misdirection and fooling the eye. I learned this from my magic book that Donell caught me reading. I think that you were right, Donell. You said that Shanna quickly tossed the shoes in the recycling shoe bin," Lily said to Donell.

"But we saw Shanna put the shoes back on the shelf," Marissa proclaimed.

"No. What we saw was Shanna putting the box on the shelf. The shoes were assumed to be in the box. But magic is about hiding things in plain sight. Watch this," Lily said.

Lily took off her shoes and placed them on the desk next to Fitz's computer. She then went over and grabbed the shoebox with the bottom cut out of it.

"Now observe casual audience members!" Lily theatrically announced.

Lily put the bottomless shoebox over her own shoes. Because it had no bottom, she slipped the box over the shoes as easily as you would slip a shirt on.

"Once the box is over the shoes, I now have to demonstrate how to lift the box and not have the shoes drop out of the bottom. I can perform this, not by holding the box," Lily said.

Fitz's eyes got wide.

"I see! You create the illusion you are carrying the box," Fitz blurted.

"Yes, Fitz, now watch as I place my hands under the box and I am holding the shoes. See?" Lily said

Lily picked up the shoebox and started walking with it.

"Wow! You look like you are carrying the shoebox," Donell said enthusiastically.

"Yes. But look! I am really holding the shoes under the box. I'm not holding the box at all," Lily told them, and showed them her hands.

The kids saw her hands holding the soles of her shoes.

"So when the front cameras were both blocked off, Shanna uses that method to take Mystic's sneakers into the backroom after quickly throwing a similar pair of shoes on the center piece. No one sees anything suspicious. The customers just see the shoe store worker returning shoes to the back room. But she would have to be quick," Donell exclaimed.

"She has some ping pong championships and she loves chess. Maybe she simply knows when to move certain pieces to her advantage and can use her quick hands," Marissa told them.

"Okay. Let's assume she made the swipe. If the shoes are not in the store, where are they?" Fitz asked Lily.

Lily smiled.

"That is where the trap door of the trick comes in. In a magic trick, to pull a disappearing act, there are trap doors and secret passageways. Peg made me think of the idea when she told me about a movie she saw. So, how can she make the shoes not appear in the store? She uses the shoe recycling bin," Lily said.

"She goes over to the recycling bin. It has a hole in the lid, or secret passage. We think that Shanna is just being vain when she looks in the mirror and plays with her hair. What she is really doing is removing her hands. She is fooling the camera. Once the hands are removed the shoes fall into the recycling bin, but the camera only picks up a box on the bin, not what is happening under it! Then the shoes just wait in the bin until they are emptied," Lily said happily.

Fitz was amazed once again. He was not the only one. All of the kids and Mr. Shultz were stunned.

"That is genius. You escape the sight of all three cameras that way! Then she picks up the now empty shoe box, and places it on the shelf. Because camera 3 is high, up it looks normal. It completely fools the camera!" Fitz shrieked.

"Wow! Lily! You did it!" Donell clapped his hands.

"We all did. We just needed to add a little magic," Lily said with a grin and a wave of her wand.

"And I just needed to have faith in some of the smartest friends someone could hope for," Donell added.

"You guys, so where are the shoes now?" Marissa asked, cutting the celebration short.

"They aren't in that stinky bin, that's for sure," Peg said.

"Well, I sent Marcus to empty the bin before I sent him home. He always does that before he leaves. He doesn't like to work much but he always insists on emptying it," Mr. Shultz replied.

"Maybe Marcus and Shanna planned it together," Donell piped in.

"And we know that the bubble gum is on the lens of Camera 4 just outside the store," added Peg.

"Yes. And that was Grape-Zillah gum. The type that Marcus likes," Lily told them.

"That's right! So Marcus empties the shoes in the yellow recycling bin outside and they can pick them up later with no camera to catch them," Fitz shouted.

"That means that the shoes could still be in the bin outside," Donell loudly exclaimed.

I'm on it!" Peg shouted.

She stormed down the steps, passing three of them. The other children moved quickly. Donell also skipped down the steps and dashed to the exit.

Donell out-raced Peg to the back of the store where earlier Peg had performed her trick. Peg threw her board down and started skating toward the bin.

"Look over there," Peg yelled.

They saw the upturned recycling bin and already down the street was a mysterious figure racing away on a bike.

"Follow that bike, Peg! They have the shoes!" Donell said.

Peg started chasing the bike down. Her feet balanced on the board and she leaned forward and kicked backwards, making the board roll faster and faster. But the biker weaved through alleyways, taking turns and curves faster than Peg could skateboard.

Peg avoided all the hazards in an attempt to keep up.

She leapt over a pipe strewn in the middle of the alley. Then she swerved to avoid some pebbles that could catch on her tires. Peg could only see the biker's back and raced to catch up.

"You have to do better than that, dude," Peg yelled.

She jumped over a puddle of water. With knobby knees bent in the air, she landed back on her board and kept following the biker. The biker swerved into another alleyway. Peg pursued.

There were many dirt patches and mounds of stringy grass overgrown through the concrete. Peg managed to avoid them as well as a barking dog springing for her. It was stopped inches away from her by a leash.

"Whoa, man! I was almost dog food," Peg cackled.

But Peg was determined not to lose the biker. When the biker turned into another street, Peg also turned. When the biker tried to lose Peg by weaving through traffic in the main street, Peg pushed on her board even harder, avoiding car bumpers, pedestrians, and cracked concrete. Peg knew the streets of Baltimore just as well as the biker.

But there were some places that a skateboard could not go that a bike could, and a park was one of them. The biker used the grass of the park and cut across the sand where the swing set and the monkey bars were. Peg could only use the squiggly walkway, and then she had to avoid power walkers, joggers, and dog walkers with their dogs.

Peg watched the biker leap over a small parking curb, bike up a seesaw, go down on the other side, then head into the street and vanish. Peg could only watch, unable to follow.

She kicked her board and caught it in her hand.

"Lucky," Peg muttered about the cyclist and sat down on her board.

She did her best to catch the culprit.

Peg pulled out her cell phone and texted Donell.

The text read: "Biker got away. I ran out of street."

Peg waited a little bit and got a response back from Marissa.

"Meet back at the Boys and Girls Community Center. We have a plan."

Peg grinned despite the disappointment in seeing the biker get away. She wished she had one of those monster skateboards that have the dirt tires. Then she could have caught that biker.

Chapter 8

Mouse-a-Phobia

The Boys and Girls Community Center was a place run by Teddy G. The kids called him that because he once took them camping in Western Maryland and his snoring was so loud the kids thought he was a bear. From then on the name stuck to him, which he gladly accepted.

Teddy G was a big man who liked to keep his ear to the streets. He was once a bad kid, but life lessons taught him that that was no way to live. So he became someone who helps his community. He worked very hard to reform his ways and when he earned enough money, he started the Boys and Girls Community Center.

Since then, the place had risen in popularity after the parents found out that Teddy G genuinely cared for the kids and worked with the parents in discipline, learning, sports and academics.

Teddy liked to keep a close ear to the streets so that he could prevent some of the bad things he experienced when he was a kid.

Until Donell, Lily, Marissa and Mr. Shultz walked in, he only knew that the Mystic Bradley sneakers had been stolen. But Donell and the gang filled him in on the clues of the case and their main suspect.

While they are all gathered around each other, Peg walked in, exhausted and sweaty from skateboarding.

"Peggy. What's good?" Teddy G said smoothly.

They were in the old recreation room. There were ping pong tables, pool tables, and an air hockey table that constantly hummed with air. There were also old arcade games like Clak Man and space shoot-off.

The rest of the kids and Mr. Shultz were around Teddy G by the faded ping pong table.

"Hey, Teddy G, what's up, man?" Peg saluted with a tired arm holding her skateboard.

"You kids have been telling me what has been going on. Said you were chasing the thief down," Teddy G said calmly. He took off his shades and smiled at Peg.

"That was really brave of you Peggy. You kids all have done a good job. Mr. Shultz and I agree that is great detective work. Now all we have to do is catch the thief with the shoes," Teddy G told them.

"Right, but how are we going to do that? If Shanna was that smart to escape all the cameras, I don't think she will let herself get caught with the shoes," Marissa added.

"She can ride, that's for sure. Anyone to out race me on my board I give mad respect to," Peg muttered.

"Marissa? Didn't you tell me Lee BMX bikes on the weekend?" Donell asked.

"He was state champion last year," Marissa said with a smile.

"So maybe Lee was working with Shanna, not Marcus. We can't really get to Shanna. She is older. But..."

"Maybe Lee will squeal," Lily piped up.

Donell thought about what Marissa told him about Lee.

"Squeal? Yes. Maybe he will," Donell replied and a smile spread across his face.

"It is worth a shot, but what about Marcus? You were so determined that he was involved," Fitz asked Donell.

"Right now Lee is a bigger suspect. And thanks to Marissa, I know there are three suspects in the case," Donell told him.

Marissa clapped her hands joyfully. Meanwhile Fitz found information about Lee on the computer.

"Lee lives on second and ninth with his Mom. I think she is a math teacher. How do we get inside to talk to him?" Fitz asked his friends.

"Leave that to me," Marissa said to them with a wink.

The next hour, Peg was wrestling with her plaid checkered skirt as Mr. Shultz dropped her and Marissa off a block away from Lee's home. They were both dressed as math cadets for S.W.A.M.P. Peg was all for the idea when Marissa suggested they could go undercover as cadets for S.W.A.M.P. Peg thought that meant donning a wet suit, and diving underwater only to come out with strands of sticky seaweed running down.

She did not know that S.W.A.M.P. was short for Strong Women's Association of Math Prowess.

So Peg sulkED down the street dressed as a math cadet of Marissa's group. The outfit was similar to Marissa's but on her beret there was a big floppy foam multiplication sign. Marissa was carrying cookies and Peg was carrying her skateboard.

"I look ridiculous," Peg moaned.

"You look better than you have ever looked Peg. I suppose you think wearing a hooded sweatshirt and scuffed shoes is any better?" Marissa teased.

"Way better," Peg sighed.

"Okay. Here we go. Are you ready, fellow math cadet?" Marissa cried.

"Ready, dude!" Peg shouted.

"No, Peg. A math cadet is proper and under control. She is balanced like an equation. Now what is our motto?" Marissa insisted.

Peg rolled her eyes.

"Math is boring, math is odd. Give me a math book, and I'll toss it out," Peg cackled.

"No. That is not it! Let's recite the motto together," Marissa corrected and came to a stop at the door.

"I know it, just knock already," Peg muttered.

Marissa smoothed her skirt and knocked on the door. She heard the sound of a dog barking and a scuttling of feet. A voice called, "Just a minute".

Lee's mother came to the door and upon seeing the math cadets, she beamed.

Peg and Marissa chanted together.

"We are math cadets and math is our game! Math is awesome and great for our brains," They sang. But Peg mixed up the chant and said "math is brains and great for our awesome".

"Hello, young cadets! Oh it is so good to see young girls interested in math! Good for you. Do come in," Lee's mother chirped.

Marissa tilted her head in thanks and confidently stepped inside. Peg followed behind, shambling, not used to heels.

She spotted a little dog perched on the staircase. It growled at her. It had a spiked collar. Peg stuck her tongue out at it, which made it mad.

"We are the math cadets of S.W.A.M.P., ma'am," Marissa beamed.

"Oh yes, yes. I am familiar. You are just in time. I have been preparing a math show for an assembly at the school for Monday. Come in. You two love math so much this will be a treat. The presentation is called, "how to make Algebra hip and hop for you," Lee's mom yelped.

"How wonderful," Marissa said.

"Yay, math," Peg groaned and they all went in the kitchen.

The little dog bounded down the steps, following them and barking shrilly at Peg.

Meanwhile, Teddy G dropped Donell and Lily off at Lee's house. Their plan was for Marissa and Peg to distract the mother while they sneak in and find Lee.

The Private Eye Five

Donell and Lily slipped out of Teddy G's car. Donell had his backpack on. Inside there were squeaking noises coming from it. Fitz offered to stay in the car and ride with Teddy.

"Thanks for allowing us to stop off at the school first, Mr. Teddy," Donell said.

"Whatever helps solve the crime, little brother," Teddy G said coolly.

"Do you want us to drive around the block?" Fitz asked Donell.

"We'll see what Lee has to say, and shoot you a text, Fitz. We might need the car to be on the move," Donell explained as Teddy let his arm rest against the window.

"Good thinking, me and Fitz will circle the block. Come on, kid genius. Let's see if you can handle my taste in music," Teddy G grinned.

They swerved back onto the street and drove off.

"Okay, Lily. Are you ready for this?" Donell asked.

"Sure thing and thanks, Donell," Lily said.

"Thank you for what Lily?" Donell replied.

"Thanks for listening to me. I know I got carried away with my magic," Lily said.

"No. I am sorry. I should have listened to you sooner. Now let's go make Mystic's shoes magically appear again," Donell cried.

Lily laughed at that.

"Like my re-appearing coin trick," She said.

The two kids crept toward Lee's house. They could see through the window. In the kitchen there was loud music playing and they saw Lee's mother dancing to a math rap. She was overheard singing, "When you have a remainder, be sure to raise it up, raise it up".

"My goodness! Poor Peg," Donell said.

They went around to the front of the house. The music was so loud they opened the door easily.

But the little dog sniffed them out. He stopped nibbling on Peg's shoes and barked loudly, chasing Donell and Lily up the steps.

"A gargoyle," Lily cried out.

"Run, Lily. It is the size of a can of tuna but look at those sharp little teeth," Donell yelped.

He was the athletic of the two and leapt up the stairway two steps at a time. But Lily skittered up the steps in clumsy strides. The little dog grabbed on to her magic cape. It yanked hard, growling in its little throat and holding its position on the stairs.

"Leave me behind, Donell, save yourself!" Lily shouted dramatically, as if she was in a movie.

Donell gritted his teeth.

"Never, Lily, we do this together," Donell said with stark determination.

The little dog was about to send Lily backwards down the steps with its wiry strength, but Donell dove for her. His glasses flew off, but he caught Lily's hand. He pulled hard and drew Lily up the steps. The little dog didn't miss a beat. It lunged at Donell. Donell could only rummage through a clothes basket blindly to find a weapon.

What he found was a long gray wooly sock with red stripes. Donell vaguely saw that the sock was already well stretched so he stretched it wider and caught the pint sized puppy in midair like a net. It wrestled inside the sock, but when it popped its head out and saw it was trapped, it stopped fighting.

"There you go, monster. A suitable cage for someone as vicious as you," Lily scolded the pup.

The little dog whimpered, stuck in the sock. Donell handed the sock to Lily who carried it with her. The dog lowered its ears sadly and in a defeated posture let its little fuzzy black paws hang limp.

'That's a good boy," Lily said and kissed the pup on the top of its little head.

"Okay. Now to find Lee," Donell said to Lily who was making cuddly faces to the puppy. He found his glasses and put them on. They were slightly crooked and bent.

They found Lee in his room down a long hall to the left. When Donell opened the door he saw Lee on his knees wiping mud off the back tires of his BMX bike. The wheel was off and the bike was flipped over so the seat was against the carpet.

"Hey Lee, what's the matter? Does your bike need a bath?" Donell interrupted.

Donell and Lily stood in the doorway, blocking the entrance.

Lee jumped with surprise when he saw Donell standing there with his arms folded.

"Donell, I didn't expect you to be here," Lee said and smiled, laughing nervously.

He wiped the dirty towel he was using over his forehead. Then he stood up and paced around the room. Donell and Lily both raised their eyebrows in unison.

"No? That is good. I thought we could have a little chat," Donell told him.

Donell motioned to Lily and Lily shut Lee's door with a slam. This made Lee jump. He glanced at Donell and then to Lily who had Lee's dog sedated in the sock.

"Hey! What did you do to Almond?" Lee cried after seeing his dog wrapped up tightly with its arms limp. The dog had fallen asleep.

"Never mind the dog. He will be fine," Lily said grimly. "Where were you just now that got your tires so dirty?"

"Nowhere, really," Lee stuttered, wiping at his brow.

Donell stooped and investigated the carpet.

"That is funny. I would say judging by the high amount of white sand on the carpet, that you were either riding your bike on the beach, which would be foolish, or you were cutting across the playground. What do you think, Lily?" Donell asked her coyly.

"I think it is something like that," Lily said.

"What are you guys getting at?" Lee sputters, fidgeting.

"Only this, Lee--we know it was you that Peg was chasing earlier today. We know you are a great biker. You would have to be, to get away from Peg. So spill the beans! Where are Mystic Bradley's stolen shoes?" Donell said, pointing a finger at Lee.

"I don't know what you are talking about Mom!" Lee cried out. But he got no answer except booming music.

"Your mother can't hear you now, Lee. She is busy downstairs with our most covert special agents," Lily said.

"You mean Peg and Marissa?" Lee asked.

"Yes, they are downstairs keeping your mother occupied with cookies that look like addition and subtraction signs and rap songs that tell you how to convert decimals to whole numbers," Lily said grimly, shaking her fist at Lee.

"You monsters," Lee whispered. His eyes bulged widely.

"It's just you and us now, Lee. So tell us where the shoes are or you'll be sorry," Donell added, scowling.

"Do your worst. You can't make me say anything," Lee laughed. He turned his back and crossed his arms.

"Okay, Lee. It's a funny thing. Marissa received rumors that one time in science class you had a panic attack. It was strange. The one moment you were fine and the next you were squeezing out the window trying to escape. What was the name he was hollering, Lily? I forgot," Donell replied.

"Squeaky, I think. But the class called him Mr. Squeaky," Lily said with a grin.

Upon hearing that dreadful name Donell unzipped his backpack and pulled out an old shoebox.

"Mr. Squeaky? No. It can't be, Donell. You wouldn't,"

Lee started begging.

"Yes Lily, that is correct. Mr. Squeaky was his name! But apparently, Mr. Squeaky was a she. And she had a bunch of little mouse babies. I visited Mrs. Squeaky today. I talked to her and told her that you would love to see her babies," Donell shook the shoebox with a grin.

The shoe box had holes cut into it. In the box there were squeaks, claw scratches and sounds of little pink feet skittering on the surface of the box. When Lee saw the box, his face drooped like a wet towel.

"No! Not that! Anything but that! I can't stand mice! I hated them ever since my parents took me to Magic Castles in Florida to see Melvin Mouse. No, please!" Lee shouted. "It would be a shame if all these mice got loose and started having thousands and millions of babies," Lily piped up. Donell started opening the lid.

"Alright! Alright! I'll talk! Yes, I took the shoes from the recycling bin! Shanna put me up to it. I don't have them now though. I dropped them off so she can sell them! Please don't release the mice! Please don't!" Lee blubbered.

'Where did you drop them off, Lee? Talk now or there will be little white mice in your cereal bowl, in your bedspread, in your closet, sitting on your bike," Lily shouted.

Donell opened the lid just enough for Lee to see little beady eyes in the dark. Lee yelped!

"No! Okay. I dropped them off at Shaggy's Sports Memorabilia. She is meeting the owner now to make the exchange. Please don't let them get in my cereal bowl," Lee sobbed.

"You are in big trouble, Lee. Why would you do something so underhandedly, anyway?" Donell asked.

Lee cleared the tears from his eyes and shook himself.

"I'm just a victim stricken by love, Donell. Surely you can understand," Lee wailed.

Donell rolled his eyes and slapped his forehead.

"No. But Fitz would. I better text him and tell him and Teddy G to get over to Shaggy's Sports Memorabilia before it's too late," Donell said, pulling out his phone.

"I already did it, Donell, and they are on their way over there," Lily uttered.

"That was quick, Lily," Donell noted.

She laughed, holding up the little dog in the sock.

"Like magic, Donell," she said to him with a smile.

Chapter 9

Tough Fitz and Shanna's Tale

"How do you like my jams, little man? Are you ready to jump out yet?" Teddy G grinned, while his music played on the radio.

He was driving quickly but safely through the busy Baltimore streets.

"It's not Kikomuko San's electric dance pop off, but it is tolerable," Fitz replied with a smile.

"Keeko? Mooky? What?" Teddy G asked.

"Kikomuko San, Mr. Teddy. They are a duo that produces ambient sound with a disco background and sound effects that are compatible with MMO games," Fitz replied.

Teddy G was laid back in his seat and maneuvering through the streets. He frowned with one hand on the steering wheel. He changed lanes expertly watching the traffic behind his shades.

"I don't know half of what you just said, little man," Teddy G said and chuckled.

"It's cool, Mr. Teddy. I like this sound too. It is good crime solving music," Fitz said and nodded his head to the rhythm.

"Great, Fitz. Hey, brother, keep doing what you're doing. You impressed Mr. Shultz with your knowledge of computers and what not," Teddy G said to Fitz.

Fitz nodded quietly, turning to Teddy, wrestling with the seatbelt so it didn't squeeze him so tightly.

"Thank you, Mr. Teddy," Fitz muttered.

"You seem nervous, brother. What is eating you?"

"Just the natural adrenaline overload of confronting a criminal, Mr. Teddy," Fitz answered. He fidgeted in his seat again.

"Are you sure? Don't worry. I will go in first. When I see that there is no danger, and then you can come in," Teddy G replied, attempting to calm Fitz's fears.

Fitz looked over at Teddy G.

"You wouldn't think of me as a poor partner?" Fitz asked.

Teddy G laughed heartily.

"You kids are the brave ones! I just got filled in. You're the detectives. You are brave, Fitz. It's cool," Teddy G added.

"I guess," Fitz weakly nodded and looked out the window. He wasn't sure that he was brave like Peg or Donell.

Teddy G turned the music down.

"You are growing up to be an intelligent and strong man. Who does your mother call now when she needs the heavy garbage bags lifted, Fitz? Teddy asked.

"Me, I guess," Fitz mumbled.

"And who does she call when there is a mouse in the house that needs catching?" Teddy asked with a wide grin? Fitz chuckled.

"My mother abhors mice. I guess that task is assigned to me as well," Fitz said, feeling a little better.

"See? You are already a good protector as a boy growing up as a man. If you weren't there to protect your mother she

might be neck deep in mice. Swimming in a sea of tails and claws..." Teddy joked.

At that image, Fitz laughed. He liked Teddy G. He had a way of talking to Fitz about things that made him feel more comfortable. But then he thought of something else.

"I still have an adequate amount of nervousness too, Mr. Teddy," Fitz told him in almost a whisper.

"I told you there is no danger, Fitz. You got me at your side," Teddy assured him.

"Maybe my nervousness doesn't altogether stem from the fear and peril of facing a criminal. Especially one, that is...very pretty," Fitz trailed off. Then he looked away and out the window.

Teddy G glanced over at Fitz. He stopped at the red light. Understanding dawned on him. He smiled. Fitz had a little crush, he realized.

"I think I see. Well, Fitz. You have to be wise in this world. We have to remember she may have stolen the shoes. Keep that in mind," Teddy G said.

"Yes. You are right, Mr. Teddy, but how can I go in there?" Teddy moaned.

Teddy G put a comforting hand on Fitz's shoulder.

"I'm here for you, little brother. We can do this together," Teddy G said and gave him a warm smile.

"The thought of it frightens me to the base of my spine to the tips of my toes," Fitz groaned.

Teddy G laughed and comforted Fitz.

"You don't have to say a word, my brother. You can be my muscle in there," Teddy told him confidently.

"How do I do that?" Fitz asked. He turned to Teddy G with curiosity forming.

"You stand behind me with your arms crossed and look real mean. Look around at the store like you smell something real bad. Trust me, if you do that, you will come off looking cool," Teddy said with an assured nod.

"Really?" Fitz questioned.

"Yes, my brother. Here. Take my shades. Yeah. They look good on you. Just nod every once in a while when you hear me say something," Teddy instructed him.

"Great, Mr. Teddy. I feel better already," Fitz said, feeling more confident.

"You have all of high school to worry about girls and stuff Fitz. For now, sit back and be my muscle," Teddy G laughed and turned the music up.

"Be your muscle. Yeah, cool just like in the movies. That sounds good," Fitz laughed and nodded his head to the beat. He loved the shades.

"That's right, little man! Here we are. Are you ready to go in here and solve this case?" Teddy asked.

Fitz unlatched his seatbelt buckle, and in his new role as tough Fitz, he nodded silently, pretending he smelled some dirty gym socks. They both stepped out of the car as crime solving partners.

Fitz slammed the door dramatically and joined Teddy as they entered Shaggy's Sports Memorabilia. The information that Lee provided didn't disappoint. There at the front counter was Shanna. She saw Teddy G and noticed the look on his face. She seemed to sense that he was not just a regular customer. Her eyes got wide.

Shaggy, the tall gangly man behind the counter wore a puzzled expression on his face. His large mop of hair covered his eyes.

"Excuse me, young lady. I have been sent to investigate a crime. What do you have in the bag?" Teddy G asked her, pointing to the bag on the counter.

"That is none of your business. Who are you, anyway?" Shanna blurted.

She clutched the bag protectively.

"I am the owner of the Boys and Girls Community Center and a volunteer officer of the Neighborhood watch. Tell me what you got in the bag," Teddy demanded.

Shanna stumbled with her words.

"Neighborhood Watch? What do you want with me? I didn't do anything!"

"We'll see about that. Maybe we'll ask Mr. Shultz, your employer about that. He is on his way right now," Teddy added. This news made Shanna tremble.

"My boss Mr. Shultz? Why is he coming here?" Shanna responded weakly.

"We know that there is a valuable pair of Mystic Bradley shoes in the bag. You either tell me and my bodyguard Fitz here, or you tell Mr. Shultz," Teddy grimaced.

Teddy G glanced at Fitz who has his arms crossed. Fitz nodded at Teddy G through his dark shades.

"Hey. We can't have you threatening our customers," Shaggy said to Teddy G in a nasal voice.

"This customer is trying to sell stolen footwear that was supposed to be auctioned for charity," Teddy G informed Shaggy.

At hearing that, Shaggy's eyes got as wide as dinner plates.

"What! She told me that she was Mystic Bradley's niece. Man! Taking money from charity? That is real cold," Shaggy scolded her in a squeaky voice.

Shanna fumed and pounded her fist on the counter.

'They are lying, Shaggy. Don't believe them," Shanna blurted out.

Shaggy shook his head. He didn't believe her story one bit.

"I don't want your business no longer," Shaggy spouted and pointed a shaking finger at her.

Shanna wheeled around toward Teddy G and Fitz.

'Now look what you have done! My uncle Mystic will be very upset that his only niece, a poor high school student that needs that money to pay for tests for college, was accosted by you," Shanna yelled.

She stomped her feet and held the bag tight to her chest.

"Stop that, Shanna," the shoe store owner's voice cut her off as he entered.

Joining him was Donell, Lily, Peg, and Marissa. They all rode back together in Mr. Shultz's station wagon.

"Cut all of the lies, Shanna. I am disappointed in you," Mr. Shultz scolded, nodding his head sadly.

Peg noticed Fitz with his arms crossed, scowling, and looking around the store.

"Hey, Fitz, looking tough, my man," Lily told him.

Fitz looked at her and silently nodded, sneaking in a smile.

Shanna, upon seeing Mr. Shultz, dropped the bag. The shoebox with the shoes spilled out.

"Mystic's shoes," Donell gasped.

"And like magic the shoes re-appear," Lily tittered and waved her magic wand.

"How did you know I was here, Mr. Shultz?" Shanna moaned, slumping down on a giant bean bag shaped like a baseball. She realized she had been defeated.

"Hey. You sit on that, you buy it," Shaggy whined and pounded his fist on the glass counter.

"I didn't find you, Shanna. I thought I might have made a mistake and lost the shoes myself. That was until Donell and his detective friends came along. They knew something was fishy," Mr. Shultz told her.

"It was real smart of you to escape all of the cameras in the store. You had us fooled. Until we realized you did it by using magic. Right, Lily?" Donell said, turning to Lily.

"That is misdirection and slight of hand," Lily piped up.

"You moved pretty quickly. You looked like a cat, but we are the dogs on the hunt," Peg muttered and nudged Fitz.

Fitz nodded silently, scanning the room.

Shanna threw her hands up and moaned.

"This is my life now? Caught by a bunch of children? How did this happen?" Shanna whined.

"You used Lee to recover the shoes, which was your greatest mistake. We used him to trace you here," Marissa spoke up.

Shanna rolled her eyes.

"Ugh! That kid would follow me everywhere. He wrote me poetry, sung me a song. He did whatever I wanted," Shanna sighed.

"Lee had a crush on you and you could make him do whatever, but what about Marcus? Was he in on the crime? What about the bubble gum on the outside camera?" Donell asked Shanna, who was slumped even lower in the bean bag.

Shanna groaned and threw her hands up in surrender.

"I guess I might as well come clean. Marcus did not help me at all. All week long he was excited to meet Mystic Bradley so I had to sneak around him. I knew he was lazy though and bet that at one point in the day he would either fall asleep or be on his phone. I was right," Shanna replied miserably.

"So why did Marcus put the gum on the camera?" Marissa asked her.

"He didn't. I did that. By using the same grape gum that Marcus loves, it was a way to frame him. So after the theft, Marcus would be blamed for putting the gum on the camera, and Lee could bike back and get the shoes without being caught. It was the perfect way of disabling all four cameras," Shanna said.

Just then, Shanna got a text, and for a minute she was distracted although she knew she was in big trouble. Everyone watched her and Shaggy paced back and forth behind his counter and scratched his chin.

Donell broke the silence.

"Wow, Marissa. You were right. It was the one we least suspected and Marcus proved to be innocent," Donell told her.

Marissa smiled at him.

"She isn't the milkman or the butler, but yes, you're right, Donell," Marissa laughed.

"Are you children done? Can we get this over with?" Shanna pleaded as she looked at her phone again.

"They may be younger than you but they are smart as whips, Shanna. These kids are real detectives," Mr. Shultz grinned and nodded at them all.

Marissa spoke up.

"We figured out how you smuggled the shoes out without anyone noticing. It was the bottomless shoe box that created the illusion. People in the store just thought you were carrying the shoebox to the back. It might have worked if Lily and Peg didn't spot your props you used to pull it off," she exclaimed, pointing her finger in the air.

The kids all grinned.

Fitz just nodded.

Donell piped in.

"Yeah. You had it down to a science. The hardest part was timing the theft with the two front cameras, but with Lee working with you, you just had to avoid Marcus. Mr. Shultz was too busy with paperwork to notice. You set up the balloons so they blocked Camera 2, then you motioned for Lee, who stretched the banner to block Camera 1. Then you stole the shoes," Donell told her.

"Okay, okay. Yes. I play chess, okay? I'm a genius, so what? I know how to manipulate pieces. Yes, the balloons, the bottomless shoebox, the mirror. Lee. Yes. I did it. Would you kids please leave me alone?" Shanna whined.

"And once you got in the backroom it was easy for you to pretend to look in the mirror as you dropped the shoes in the recycling bin," Lily spoke up happily, ignoring Shanna's frustrated expressions.

"Great. Fine. I don't know how you kids figured it out, but I am completely over it," Shanna told them and started texting.

"Because we had a great magician on our team," Donell shouted happily, which made all of them cheer except Shanna.

"You are in big trouble, kid. Mr. Shultz and I are going to go talk to your parents. By the time you are out of your room from being grounded, you will have gray hair," Teddy G scolded her.

"Whatever," Shanna said.

"Why did you do it, Shanna?" Mr. Shultz asked.

"Because I could use the money, Mr. Shultz. Five hundred dollars could have gone a long way," she uttered.

"Yes. For a new prom dress, I bet," Marissa said with a sly grin.

"Well, your crime is going to go a long way, too. This will go on your school record and it will be hard for you to be accepted in any colleges. You are going to have to work extra hard now to get ahead," Teddy warned her.

"I guess I didn't think that I would get caught. When I saw

that Lee was going to do anything for me, I came up with

the plan. I met Shaggy, and told him I was Mystic's niece,

and it was settled," Shanna said.

"I can't believe I fell for such a hair-brained story. I'm

glad you kids solved the mystery. I love mysteries,"

Shaggy shouted.

"You can tell Mystic you have his shoes now, Mr. Shultz,"

Donell said.

"I'm on the phone with him right now, Donell. I think it is

too late to hold the event, though," Mr. Shultz said.

"Too bad you didn't't get to see Mystic, Donell," Lily told

him.

Donell shrugged.

"You know what? I was so upset I couldn't see him that I

didn't even think about why Mr. Shultz was holding the

event. He did it to promote a charity to encourage kids to read. It took this whole shoe incident to make me realize that. I was selfish, guys. I wanted to see Mystic Bradley so bad I didn't see the bigger picture," Donell told them.

"I'm going to cry like when my mom watches soap operas," Shanna uttered, waiting for her parents, who were called by Shaggy. She was definitely in big trouble.

"Hey, Donell, I told Mystic about what you kids have done and he wants to talk to you," Mr. Shultz called, holding his phone by his ear.

"Me! Mystic Bradley wants to talk to me?" Donell uttered in amazement.

Chapter 10

An Agency is formed with Friendship

Donell and the gang solved the crime, but did not do it in time to make the deadline for the auction. But Mystic was so glad about the kid's detective work and recovering the shoes, that he planned on a big special event. When Donell heard about what Mystic Bradley was designing, his jaw almost dropped to the floor. He was in such a state of shock, he couldn't talk for minutes.

After Donell recovered, he enthusiastically informed everyone they were invited to see Mystic Bradley play against the Boston Bomb Cats, one of the biggest rivals of the Baltimore Bay Birds.

They were in the stands, in the third row watching Mystic Bradley slam dunk after spinning off a defender. The crowd was cheering and waving their banners. The kids were smiling from ear to ear.

The big speakers boomed. The smell of popcorn and hotdogs and sweaty sneakers -wafted through the Baltimore Arena. Every time Mystic scored, the sound system produced a sound effect like stars twinkling, as if a magic spell had been cast.

"Mystic has the magic touch," the announcer on the loud speaker proclaimed.

This made Lily smile. She wasn't wearing her magic robe but she did have her wand in her hand.

Donell was sitting beside her. He could hardly believe he was so close to the action. He could see the coach jumping up and down and running the sidelines, yelling at his players. He could see all the times the players went back to the bench and discussed strategy during timeouts.

But the best thing about it was that Donell was with his crime solving buddies and best friends. He learned a lot of important lessons, but the main one was to listen to his friends.

Donell looked down the row.

Beside Lily, Fitz was watching the game on his phone so he could follow the statistics. Next to him, Peg was shoving two hotdogs into her mouth. Then there was Marissa, Mr. Shultz, and Teddy G. Mystic Bradley was adamant that he wanted everyone there who had helped with the case.

The kids were having so much fun, cheering loudly for Mystic Bradley and the Birds.

But the night was about to get even better for Donell and his detective friends.

At halftime, after the cheerleaders and mascots performed, Mystic Bradley walked out to the center of the court. To the shock of Donell and the gang, he motioned for all of them to join him. Peg had to nudge Donell to get him out of his seat.

The kids joined Mystic in the center of the floor. He was so tall; all the kids had to look way up to see his big beaming smile. Mystic had a microphone in his hand so he could be heard by the whole arena.

Mystic told the audience that the kids led the way in the case of the stolen sneakers.

The Private Eye Five

Donell wiped his glasses. The crowd was cheering loudly for the kids.

Mystic allowed the kids to receive the applause and then raised his long arms for silence.

He spoke.

"Now I know that I should be in the locker room at halftime. But I have to let you all know how great these kids are who are standing up here before me tonight. With the help of Mr. Shultz the shoe store owner, and Teddy G the owner of the Boys and Girls Community Center, they solved a crime so that I can donate my shoes to the Inner Harbor Children's Literacy Fund. Together, they used all of their talents and figured it out! Let's give them a great big hand," Mystic urged.

The crowd roared like an ocean wave.

Teddy G and Mr. Shultz smiled widely and shook hands with one another.

Mystic grinned.

Peg raised her hands in the air, accepting the powerful waves of applause. Fitz nodded his head at the audience. Lily stood in shock at the large crowds, and Marissa did a little petite bow. Donell waved at the audience.

Mystic got down on one knee. He was now face to face with Donell.

"Donell, I understand that you are one of my biggest fans. I think that deserves a special reward. Not only am I going to give you a free pair of the new Mystic Big Air Sneakers with my autograph. I am also going to give you all a chance to play against me right now. I am challenging you and all your intelligent friends. The first team to score a point wins. What do you say?" Mystic asked.

Donell could only mutter in amazement. His world spun around him. He could never have thought this would happen in his wildest dreams. But Mystic was asking to play basketball with him. He nodded his head in agreement but was in a daze.

In mere seconds, Donell took to the court. Teddy G shouted for Donell to put it on him. Mr. Shultz didn't understand what has happening, so Teddy G happily told Mr. Shultz that all of the kids were going to play against Mystic Bradley and the first one to put the ball in the basket would be the winner.

"That sounds easy if the kids have a step ladder," Mr. Shultz smiled and nodded.

The kids had the ball first. They passed it back and forth while Mystic ran the court, pretending to defend them. He moved slow on purpose, allowing Fitz to leisurely dribble by him. Peg jumped up and down and begged for the ball. Fitz passed it to her in four bounces.

Peg ran with the ball, avoiding dribbling, and carrying it more like a football. Mystic pretended to chase her and acted like he couldn't grab it from her. Peg passed it to Marissa. Marissa, who was a very good athlete as well, dribbled it to the middle. Then she passed to Lily.

Lily barely touched it before putting it on the ground and kicking it to Donell.

This made the crowd laugh and cheer.

Then they were yelling for Donell to shoot it.

And then it was just Donell. He was playing against his hero Mystic Bradley and had a chance to win a game against him. He had an open jump shot just beyond the foul line. Mystic was running towards him and grinning.

"Shoot it, Donell," Fitz screamed.

"Shoot it, dude," Peg shouted.

"Put his eye out," Teddy G stood up and yelled.

"Yes. Out with his eye," Mr. Shultz yelled along with Teddy G.

Donell planted his feet, bended his knees, jumped and released the basketball into the air. Mystic pretended to swipe at it and barely missed it with his fingertip. The ball sailed up and over and through the net! Donell made the shot!

The Private Eye Five

The scoreboard lit up and Donell and his gang were declared the winner. Mystic shrugged his wide shoulders and grabbed the microphone.

"These kids are too good. You see what teamwork can do, ladies and gentleman? They just beat me in my own sport," Mystic laughed.

Donell and the gang gathered around and gave each other hugs and high fives. Although Mystic Bradley was only pretending to play defense, it still felt great when the ball went seamlessly through the net and the crowd roared.

Mystic declared on the microphone.

"Wow! What a team!"

The whole event seemed like a dream to Donell and he was still in a daze for a few hours after the game while sitting at the dinner table with his Dad and Mom. They let Donell know that they were extremely proud of him. His mom fixed his favorite meal—spaghetti with monster meatballs and garlic bread. Donell ate happily and went right to bed, unable to believe what happened over the course of the day.

The other kids also went back to their homes where they soaked up the events of that crazy Saturday.

Life seemed to go back to normal after the weekend, until they saw the headline in the school paper written by Marissa Gonzalez. The headline said:

Crack Pot Team of Kid Detectives Solve Case!

On the cover were Donell, Lily, Fitz, and Marissa, all smiling as Mystic Bradley stood over them.

The article went on to explain how Donell and the group solved the crime of the stolen Mystic Bradley sneakers. Marissa wrote a good piece. It told their full names and even their area of expertise in helping to solve the crime.

The newspaper article said that Donell was the Scene Investigator. He was responsible for gathering clues from witnesses and walking the streets for clues.

"But I suspected the wrong person," Donell said, when confronted later by Marissa.

"You were still brave, Donell. You brought us together. You are definitely a great investigator—so no arguments Mister," Marissa said and pointed a finger at Donell.

Donell backed away and grinned. He knew not to cross Marissa when she was determined.

"Okay. Scene Investigator it is," Donell chuckled.

Fitz was considered the technical investigator in the article, to which he nodded silently and glanced around the room with his hands in his pockets. Apparently he still was acting like the muscle.

"That works for me," Fitz said with a smirk.

Peg was the enforcing investigator, as the article highlighted how bravely she put herself into action, following Lee on his bike.

"Alright. Cool, man. Criminals beware," Peg hollered.

"What about me?" Lily said.

Marissa grinned and pointed to the article.

"The report says that you discovered a non-conventional way to solve the crime, Lily. That makes you a special investigator," Marissa told her.

"Whoa! Very cool," Lily said and clapped her hands.

She loved the title and was already imagining taking on cases involving ghosts, space pirates, and third dimensions.

"What are you, Marissa?" Donell asked as Marissa strolled away.

Marissa turned and shrugged her shoulders.

"I didn't do too much. All I did was use my friends and

special groups to find out about the suspects. No biggie," Marissa told them.

"That sounds like a big deal to me. I would call you our research investigator. What do you think, Marissa? Do you want to join our group of crime solvers?" Donell asked.

Lily, Fitz, and Donell encouraged her and nodded.

"Well that depends. Would it interfere with my impeccable grades, my responsibilities in the drama club, the math cadets, the weaving foundation, or my dance class?" Marissa asked.

Donell grinned and laughed loudly.

"Nope. All of those clubs and groups you are part of make you the best choice for this group," he told her.

"Thanks. But my first responsibility is to build my college resume," Marissa told them.

"I can see 'research analyst for small crime investigation' a good thing to add to it, Marissa," Donell said.

"Oh, yes. I never thought about that! That will show my networking skills, my research prowess, my overall work ethic, and my firm stance for justice. Okay. I'm in," Marissa chirped and jumped in the air.

After school, the kids celebrated their new group meeting at the Boys and Girls Community Center. They gathered in the old recreation room playing air hockey and drinking Fuzzy Pop.

Teddy G strolled in, smiling calmly. He had a rag and some cleaner.

"Hey. What's good?" He greeted them warmly.

"Nothing, Mr. Teddy. We are forming a group to solve crimes, and are in the planning process," Fitz said.

"Like a detective agency? Hey, if any kids can pull it off, then you all could," Teddy told them.

"You don't think it would be a waste of time?" Marissa asked.

"No way, think about all the things you learned from the last case. You learned to be observant in the smallest details," Teddy said.

"Yeah, that's right," Donell added.

"You learned about the importance of teamwork. Not one of you alone could have solved the case. It took all of you to do it. That is a big lesson," Teddy said.

"We also learned that you can't judge a book by its cover. Shanna was a damsel that walked upon the clouds outwardly but when we met her she was smellier than the inside of a pair of sweaty sneakers," Fitz exclaimed.

Teddy G laughed at that image. He nodded and agreed.

"I also learned that Marcus wasn't as bad as I thought he was," Donell said.

"Yeah, just because someone treats you bad does not mean that we can instantly judge them for a crime. We need to know for sure," Peg said.

"That's right, Peg. Marcus might bully you guys sometimes, but he was cool this time," Teddy G said.

He started wiping down the arcade machines.

"I learned that there are bigger things in life than getting an autograph and playing basketball. Kids loving books and learning how to read is greater than meeting my favorite basketball star," Donell told them.

"I learned that being different from everyone does not mean that I am less important to the group. A wise old man taught me that," Lily added, thinking about Dices.

"Yeah, without Lily's awesome imagination we would have never solved the crime," Donell exclaimed.

"I learned that math can be very scary especially when it dances around in the kitchen to hip hop music and high heels," Peg said and cackled.

The gang laughed with her.

"I can make math really fun for you, Peg. Maybe I'll invite you to the next S.W.A.M.P. meeting," Marissa teased her playfully.

"I'm not falling for that again," Peg blurted.

"See all the things you learned. I think opening up your own detective agency would be a great way to grow as young adults," Teddy exclaimed.

"I guess we can meet at my house. We just have to sit on the couches with plastic or my mom will flip," Fitz remarked.

"No way, let's have it at my house," Peg protested.

"I have met your older brother and after him, being bullied by Marcus would be an utter pleasure," Fitz said.

"We can't have it at my house unless you want to change diapers and clean up after toddlers all day," Marissa remarked.

"Maybe we can have it at my house guys?" Donell suggested.

"You live so far from all of us. We don't all skate like Peg," Lily said.

"Dude, that is a long way," Peg whistled.

When a solution could not be met, Teddy G spoke up.

"Kids, how would you like to run your office right out of this place? You can have this old recreation room. We can set you up with desks, computers, and even a big white board for brain storming," Teddy G told them.

"Whoa! That would be great," Marissa joyfully announced.

They all agreed excitedly and chattered about what the next steps will be.

So Donell and the kids set up their detective agency in the old recreation room in Teddy G's Boys and Girls Community Center. It was convenient because it was close to school and when their parents were at work, they often went there anyway to unwind, do their homework, and enjoy sports and games.

It took a lot of hard work but after some hammers, nails, drills and decorating, the detective agency was open for business. The fame of Mystic Bradley and Marissa's report gave the kids the advertising to cause a stir among the community.

The End

Epilogue

The fact is that there are tons of crimes out there committed every day. It takes some smart and creative kids to catch the culprits. Join them on their adventures. They are sure to be some cases that may baffle the smartest detectives. Can you pay attention to the details and help them solves their cases? I know you can!

Made in the USA
Lexington, KY
06 November 2017